GODS AND TITANS: BATTLE FOR
EARTH First edition. November 9, 2024.

Written by Zachary Zahara

GODS AND TITANS: BATTLE FOR EARTH

By: Zachary Zahara

TO GET THE FULL IMMERSION OF THIS
STORY,
I SUGGEST LISTENING TO MY ALBUMS
"CALL OF THE OLYMPIANS" AND
"REIGN OF THE TITANS" WHILE
READING. BOTH OF THESE ALBUMS
ACT AS A SOUNDTRACK TO THIS BOOK.
ENJOY THE STORY. **-ZACK**

Table of Contents:

INTRODUCTION

Before we jump into the story, I understand that not everyone is versed in the tales of Greek Mythology. Hades, most people don't realize that the religion still exists. Because of this, I've decided to write a brief crash course on the bits significant to this book. I can't go over every detail of Greek Mythology, however, because, there's just too much for a short introduction.

It's important to note that Greek Mythology was eventually adopted by the Romans, who had a strange mix of pantheons, mainly Greek, before the start of Christianity. The Romans kept the general concepts from the Greeks but changed the names and some behaviors of the deities, as well as tweaked various aspects of these stories. In this introduction, I will give you both the Greek and Roman names of these deities, as they are important to note in my story. I've also added an index at the end that lists each deity and creature that appears in the book.

Our story begins at the dawn of time, where there was nothing but an empty void in space, known as "Chaos". From this Chaos, Gaea (Terra to the Romans) was born. Gaea was known as Mother Earth and gave birth to many of the first deities in Greek Mythology. From Gaea, came Uranus, also known as Father Sky. Even though Uranus was technically the son of Gaea, he also, in typical Greek Mythology fashion, became her husband. Eros (Cupid to the Romans) was born from Uranus and became the god of love. After Eros, Chaos created two more deities: Tartarus and Erebus (Scotus to the Romans). Tartarus is the equivalent of the Christian Hell, while the dead pass through Erebus. All of these deities above are referred to as the Primordial Gods.

The next line of deities came from these Primordial Gods. Specifically, most came from

Gaea and Uranus. Their first brood are known as the Titans. Gaea and Uranus gave birth to 12 Titans, which comprised of 6 males and 6 females: Kronus (Saturn), Oceanus, Iapetus (Japetus), Hyperion, Krios (Crius), Koios (Coeus), Tethys, Themis (Justitia), Theia (Dione), Rhea (Ops), Phoebe and Mnemosyne (Moneta).

Sometime after these initial 12 Titans, came monsters called Hecatoncheires (Centimani), or the "Hundred-Handed Ones". The Hecatoncheires were giants like the Titans, but they were known for being much uglier and monstrous. The Hecatoncheires were named Gyges, Cottus, and Briareus. After the Hecatoncheires, Gaea also gave birth to the first Cyclopes named Arges, Brontes, and Steropes. Some refer to these as the "Master Cyclopes".

Uranus thought that the Hecatoncheires were so horrifyingly grotesque that even hiding them inside Gaea, which he originally did, wasn't enough to satisfy him. So, to rid himself of these beasts, Uranus banished the Hecatoncheires to Tartarus. Tartarus then became the place where banished monsters, Gods, and Titans would wind up.

Gaea, however, did not like this decision made by her husband. She disdained Uranus so much that she started plotting her revenge almost instantly. Gaea forged a scythe worthy of killing a god. She then brought together her Titan children and devised a plan to castrate Uranus. Kronus was determined to be the one who would carry out the deed. The Titans and Gaea trapped Uranus, making him unable to move, while Kronus executed their plan. When this was done, Kronus, now King of the Titans and all beings, cast the genitals of Uranus far into the oceans. This caused the birth of Aphrodite (Venus), Meliae (tree nymphs), Erinyes (the furies), and more giants.

With Kronus now ruling over everything, he needed a queen. Kronus took Rhea as his bride. Between Kronus and Rhea came the first six of the next generation of gods, who would later be known as the Olympians. These Olympians were: Hestia (Vesta), Demeter (Ceres), Poseidon (Neptune), Hera (Juno), and Zeus (Jupiter). Hades (Pluto) was the first-born son of Kronus. While he is just as powerful and just as important as his siblings, he is not *technically* an Olympian. Hades is also sometimes used as the name of the Underworld, which you shall see in the novel ahead. However, before these new gods were born, Kronus received a prophecy from Uranus's spirit. The prophecy stated that one of Kronus's children would end his rule, killing him and taking the throne. Out of fear of losing his power and status, Kronus decided to swallow each of his children whole when they were born.

Rhea was furious about the acts of Kronus. To spite her husband, on the day of Zeus's birth, Rhea switched baby Zeus out with a rock and sent him away to the island of Crete. The unsuspecting Kronus swallowed the rock Rhea presented him, thinking it was his newest child. Zeus grew up on

Crete and, when he came of age, returned home to free his brothers and sisters from the gut of their father. After releasing his older siblings, as well as the Hecatoncheires and Cyclopes from Tartarus, the great war started.

The Olympians waged war on the Titans for 10 long and disastrous years. With the help of special weapons forged by the Master Cyclopes and Titans who joined their cause, the Olympians were victorious. Kronus and all the opposing Titans were then sent to the depths of Tartarus, where they would spend the rest of their days.

The defeat of the Titans left a huge power vacuum in the world. This vacuum needed to be divided and split up between the new rulers of the cosmos. Zeus, the savior of the Olympians and leader of the battle, became the new King of the Gods and the god of the skies (specifically lightning). Poseidon became the god of the seas, Hades the god of the underworld, Hera the goddess of marriage, Aphrodite the goddess of love,

Demeter the goddess of the harvest, and Hestia the goddess of the hearth.

Eventually, the rest of the Olympians were born from the original five. Although, they were mainly from Zeus and his many affairs and marriages. Hermes (Mercury), son of Zeus and Maia, became the messenger of the gods. The twins Artemis (Diana) and Apollo were born from Zeus and Leto. Artemis became the goddess of the hunt and wildlife. Apollo became the god of music, medicine, and prophecy. Apollo is often times known as the sun god as well, interchanged with Helios (Sol) who is the Titan god of the sun. Artemis, in turn, also occasionally takes Selene's (Luna) duties over the moon. Ares (Mars), son of Zeus and Hera, became the god of war. Athena (Minerva), daughter of Zeus and Metis, became the goddess of wisdom and war strategy. Persephone (Proserpina), daughter of Zeus and Demeter, became the goddess of vegetation. Hephaestus (Vulcan), son of Zeus and Hera, became the god of the forge. Last but not least, Dionysus (Bacchus), son of Zeus and Semele, became the god of wine and madness.

      There are many other minor gods and stories of the misadventures they all share. However, this is where I leave the introduction and jump into our main story. This story takes place many millennia after the original birth of the gods. The story of the second great war...

Chapter 1: Juno's Wedding

Nerves are running through my body, firing on all cylinders. This needs to be perfect. Everything must be in the right place, correct positioning, and *nothing* out of order. I am the goddess of marriage, after all, and this is the wedding of all weddings. The king of the gods and the queen of the gods rejoin in union once more.

Our family will be here for the reception. I charged Venus with seating arrangements. She's up to date on all the gossip around Olympus and knows who not to have at the same table. Sol gave us the perfect sunny day; not too hot but not too cool. The sun shines perfectly on the garden. Ah, the garden of Ceres. So beautiful and full of life. The perfect place for the perfect wedding. However, it is unfortunate that her daughter, Proserpina, is stuck in the underworld this time of year with her husband Pluto. Ceres, while trying to maintain her composure, is clearly in no celebratory mood. Poor thing, always trapped in a cycle of depression.

As I walk down the aisle, Apollo and his muses play the most exquisite set of songs. I never was too fond of the young god, with him being a spawn of one of my husband's many affairs, but I have to say his musical talents are unparalleled. The gods and the assortment of mythical creatures are all in high spirits. Venus did a wonderful job with the seating, it seems.

My husband and I shall sit at the frontmost table, accompanied by Apollo, Diana, and Neptune. The next table has Vulcan, Minerva, Vesta, and Mercury. At the final main table sat Mars, Bacchus, Ceres, and Venus herself. Funny how she chooses to sit with Mars instead of Vulcan. Even when I say "no drama" that girl always has to sprinkle in some.

But that's alright, I can't get mad at my officiary on the wedding day.

I finally make it down the aisle. My darling husband, Jupiter, is standing there awaiting my arrival. He's dressed in the same suit he always wears. A deep blue and gray color with little golden lightning bolts as his cufflinks. I wish he'd try something else after all of our marriages but I'll take what I can get. At least his long white hair and beard are cleaned up.

Venus stands there with him. She's wearing the most beautiful dress I have ever seen, besides mine of course. Pink cherry blossom flowers dance around the bottom of her red dress. She always knows how to dress for the occasion. Her heterochromic eyes so full of life as she looks to me.

Now, it's time for the wedding ceremony to commence. Venus reads out her favorite passages and poems about love and union. I picked out some of my own favorites about family and marriage, which she reads beautifully. As usual, however, she goes a little off-script. She springs into a huge lecture on happiness and love.

"Venus, sweetie, you're doing it again," Vulcan shouts from his seat. I wish he had done something about his ugly singed eyebrows and would just fully shave his hair already. Better to be bald than having tufts of patchy hair. At least he's ditches his jeans and apron for something proper. He even has shirt on this time.

"Oh, alright." Venus waves off his comments, "I'll stop if it's that much of a bother."

"Oh, stop it. You always get so sensitive about these things."

"Well excuse me for being the goddess of love! Unlike you, I enjoy my job!" My head turns back and forth between the quarreling couple. Venus looks as if she's ready to pounce on him. Her flowing pink hair moving slightly out of place as they argue.

A huge grinding sound fills the air as Vulcan jumps out of his seat. "It's not the job that I hate! It's that damn volcano! Do you know how hot that place gets?"

"Oh you poor thing, please tell me more. You only mention it every time we talk." Venus changes her voice to try and mock Vulcan's, "It's like 2,000 degrees in this place, sweetie. Babe, do you know how much we sweat in here? Don't even get me started on these useless cyclopes!"

Of course now Neptune chimes in, "Hey! I lent you those cyclopes! If you don't like them then give them back!" His hair is strikingly similar to my husbands, but with a teal color and singular braid in his beard. His green eyes are as wild and ferocious as the oceans he commands.

Vulcan aggressively points his finger at Neptune "Don't you butt into this, sea god!"

I can feel my face grow red hot with anger, my fists closed tightly around the bouquet I'm holding. "I will *NOT* have your petty grievances ruin my wedding! Sit down and be silent!"

"Ha! You're one to talk about pettiness, Juno. Which one of Jupiter's bastards are you ruining the life of now?" Neptune leans back in his chair and scoffs.

"SILENCE!" The disrespectful comment causes my husband to finally lose his temper. His eyes spark with frustration. "Venus, continue with the ceremony, without the tangents please." Jupiter adjusts his suit and tie nervously and he turns his attention back to me.

"Right, apologies, Lord Jupiter." Venus goes back to her spot on the altar as Vulcan returns to his seat. "Now you will each say your vow-"

"Skip the vows, let's get this over with. I need a drink." I snap back at her.

"Oh, okay." Venus continues, making sure to stick to the script this time, "Well then I now pronounce you husband and wife. You may now kiss the bride?" She spoke that last part almost as if it were a question. Maybe my husband and I were a little too harsh. I will talk to Venus later but right now, this wedding is all that matters.

Jupiter leans in and places his lips on mine. As we kiss, we seal our marriage and vows once more. The hairs on his face tickle mine as he pulls me in. Like always, his kiss sends tiny bolts of electricity through my body. I hope that, in some ways, I do the same to him. Our friends and family clap and cheer with excitement, giving a roaring applause that could be heard worldwide. We did it. We are married. The time to celebrate will come later, but first, we must make an announcement.

"Everyone, my wife and I have something we would like to say." Jupiter motions for me to take the stage.

"Yes," I continue, "Jupiter and I... we are with child." I place my hands over my stomach, and Jupiter places his hands on top of mine.

"There will be a new god born of this world soon: a new member of our very, very dysfunctional family," Jupiter says, proudly looking over at me with a stupid grin. I never could resist that face.

To my surprise, Hercules rushes up to the altar in excitement. "A new brother? This is great news, father! I'm so happy for you both!" He seems genuinely excited for us even after everything I put him through when he was a mortal. It was...touching.

In good faith for the wedding and new beginnings, I hold back my disdain for my husband's bastard and return the pleasantries.

"Thank you, Hercules. We do not yet know of the baby's gender, as we chose to leave this one as a surprise."

Neptune rushes up next, pulling his brother to the side. "Brother, a quick word please?" I listen in on their whispers.

"Of course. What is it, Neptune?" Jupiter goes along with him.

"Well, it's just that... I thought you banned the gods from having any more children. Now you're announcing that you and Juno are expecting?"

Jupiter places his hand on Neptune's shoulder for reassurance. "Fear not, brother. This, while unexpected when I first heard the news, will be fine. We are in peaceful times now. One more deity won't hurt."

"That's not what I mean. Jupiter, don't get me wrong. I'm happy for you both, and I support this. However, the other gods-"

"Will also support their king and queen or keep their opinions to themselves. They will not dare to cross me." The storms of the sky can be seen in Jupiter's eyes as his tone shifts drastically.

"Of course, brother." Neptune puts on a fake smile. He gives me a small "congratulations" on his way past me. I will have to speak to Jupiter about their conversation later.

Venus, blooming with excitement, announces to the uneasy crowd. "This is cause for celebration! Our king and queen have not only wed this day but announced the birth of a new deity! I say we take this celebration to my, um, *club* as the mortals call it. What say you?" She turns to Jupiter and I.

"Well, I think that that is a lovely idea. I did say I need a drink." It was true, after all the work put into today, and the random drama, I am in need of a good drink.

"It is decided then. Gods, goddesses, and everything in between: join us at this club for a celebration!" Jupiter shouts with his hands stretched out to the crowd.

"Now that is the best thing I've heard all day!" Bacchus eagerly jumps to his feet, knocking over his already empty bottles of wine.

All the attendees stand and cheer for their king and queen one last time. They are also probably excited for the excuse to party. Deities love a good festivity, after all. We decide to head to Venus's club immediately, without wasting a moment.

Chapter 2: Club Venus; Gods Celebrate

The club is booming, as it does every night. The music is blaring, neon lights are flashing in sync with the beat, and people are dancing. A few years ago, Bacchus and I decided it was high time for us to enter the club scene. In doing so, we created the best nightclub humanity has ever experienced. A place where humans and the divine can party amongst one another freely. Except, the humans don't know that part. We aptly named it Club Venus. Only the hottest musicians play here and only the strongest liquor is served, with a shot of nectar mixed into it for that extra kick. Not a single person leaves Club Venus unsatisfied, we make sure of that.

As soon as we arrive, the energy of the club increases exponentially. Many people believe that we Olympians hate humans and wish to see them suffer. In reality, it's quite the opposite. We take every chance we get to mingle with humans and study their ways. Humans fascinate us. Hades, it's the reason why Bacchus and I made this club in the first place.

While most of the gods and goddesses are partying on the dance floor and the bar, Jupiter, Juno, Mars, and I sit down at the VIP table. We mainly just stayed in our wedding outfits, no need to change until duty calls. We're having a wonderful time: laughing, sharing stories, and messing with random mortals in the club. Even Juno, who is usually seen as stuck-up, is letting herself go and enjoying the moment. Sometimes even we deities need a moment of relaxation. A moment of reprieve from our duties. There are other pantheons to cover, after all.

I watch Mercury swipe a bottle from behind the bar and run towards our table. His blue eyes gleem almost as bright as his father's. "This place is wonderful!" Mercury exclaims between breaths, right before taking another swig of nectar and zooming away to the dance floor. That boy never could stay still for too long.

"Though I think he's annoying, even when he's sober, I'm inclined to agree with him. This place is great, Venus." Mars, brushing back his shoulder-length black hair, glances across the table at me. His eyes, while fearsome to most, always seem warm whenever I gaze upon them. They have a deep red tint, probably from all the bloodshed he's seen. Most people assume that, as a war god, he'd walk around stiff and angry. That couldn't be more wrong. He knew when it was time to be ruthless, and when it was time to let loose.

You might be thinking "Aren't you married to Vulcan?", while the simple answer is yes, the real answer is more complicated than that. Years ago,

Vulcan "won" my hand in marriage. I had no choice. It was either I marry that greasy pig or face the wrath of Jupiter. But one does not constrain the goddess of love. Love goes, where love wants.

"Thank you, Mars. I can't take all the credit, however. Bacchus," I point over to Bacchus who is chugging from a keg with a group of club-goers, "he helped me make this place into what it is." As always, his shirt is stained from the wine; the liquid dripping in his small beard. I can never tell what he's thinking. All you get when you look in his eyes is a glimpse of what I can only describe ass broken christmas lights. Nothing but chaos behind them. A ring made of vines is weaved through his short black hair.

"Well, it is lovely. I can't think of a better place to celebrate my wedding. Don't you think so, honey?" Juno raises her wine glass to her lips, taking a small sip as she leans close to Jupiter.

Liquid spills down Jupiter's chin and onto his shirt as he tries to answer while chugging a can of beer. Like father like son I suppose. He wipes his mouth, "Yes, of course! The liquor here is quite spectacular, did you put nectar in this?"

"In every brew." I can't help but chuckle.

The conversation continues for a while longer. Roaring laughter and petty arguments occur throughout the night as drunken gods and goddesses leave and join the table. Soon everyone is drunk enough to be on the dance floor, mingling with the mortals. Anytime Jupiter gives notice to a young female, Juno shoots him a death stare. Some things never change, even among the divine.

I watch from an overhanging balcony, making sure all my guests are having fun. Apollo walks off stage after his set and rushes to his sister, Diana, who is in no dancing mood. Currently, she's sitting alone at the VIP table drinking in disgust. Her bow sits beside her. While she still brought her weapon, I guess I can be thankful she isn't dressed in her normal camo hunting gear. She even got her hair done. Normally she reminds me of Jupiter with the long messy white hair.

"Sister!" He sings in a melodic tone while twirling before sitting next to her. "Why are you brooding by yourself? Are you not enjoying the festivities?" Their dark blue eyes lock.

She crosses her arms, sinking into her seat. "I hate clubs, Apollo, you know that." That she does. I can understand why she has always seemed uncomfortable in these places. Why she and her followers never visit here outside of special events. But she tries. She showed up today, after all.

Apollo pours himself a drink from one of the bottles of nectar on the table. "I do? I mean... Oh yeah! Of course! You hate clubs because of... the uhh..."

"Because it's the perfect hunting ground for men to get defenseless women drunk or drugged so that they can have their way with them like the pigs they are." Diana clutches her bow and looks around the club. I always admired how protective she can be.

"Yeah... that..." Apollo nervously took a sip from his cup. "You know, Diana, while I agree with you and your drunken rants, you should still try to enjoy yourself. That kind of stuff can't happen here. Venus simply would not allow something like that to happen in her presence and you know that. It's okay to let loose a little and have fun for once." He's right. Like Diana, I can be protective too. Maybe that's why she and I get along so well. We have our differences, sure, but we also share common interests.

Diana loosens her grip on her bow. "Maybe you're right. I have seen what Venus does to those types of people. It's even worse than what I do."

Apollo stands up, raises his arms, and walks back into the crowd of people. He shouts over his shoulder, "I know I'm right! When am I ever wrong?!"

"Screw it." Diana chugs the rest of her drink and follows her brother into the crowd of people on the dance floor. Now this could be interesting.

Speaking of interesting, on another side of the club, an unlikely duo is dancing together. Neptune and Minerva have a long history of hatred and rivalry. However, tonight, it seems as though they are deciding to leave all that in the past and enjoy the moment. They must've had too much to drink. Neptune holds Minerva close as they dance to the sound of the music booming in their ears.

Neptune cracks a smile. "You know, Minerva, I didn't expect to be dancing with you of all goddesses tonight."

"Finally something we agree on. You'd think as the goddess of wisdom I'd know better than to dance with my rival." She teases him, returning the grin. It's nice to see them getting along. Maybe her high ponytail isn't tied as tightly as usual. She's also traded in her emerald gaintlets for cute emerald bracelets and a beautiful necklace.

"Well, I will say this: it's a nice change of pace. All those years of pointless fighting we did. The feeling of getting revenge never felt as good as this moment right now." Neptune gazes into Minerva's gray eyes.

As they dance to the music, Minerva rests her head on Neptune's chest. Her black hair blends into his long beard. "It might be the nectar talking but I agree. Don't get any funny ideas though, sea god."

"Not even in your wildest dreams, Minerva." Neptune jests back.

We gods and goddesses party the night away. So much so that Bacchus had to restock the bar more than once. It's truly a night to be remembered, even for the eternal lives of us Olympians. Of course, no Olympian gathering is complete without fights but overall spirits remain high. Unfortunately, with all that drinking comes one nasty hangover even the divine can't escape...

I walk through the aftermath of the night's events. Bottles are everywhere, tables are destroyed, and all the Olympians are sleeping on my floor. Typical signs of a great night. Apollo stumbles out of the seat he had fallen asleep in, to his right is a young mortal woman, and to his left a mortal man around the same age. As usual, he looks grumpy and annoyed to be awake. He knows that it's time to fulfill his duties as the sun god.

I notice all the other Olympians passed out around the club. Jupiter and Juno are slumped together in the VIP booth. Neptune and Minerva seem to have crashed behind the bar, and the rest scattered around randomly. It looks like the aftermath of a frat party.

I walk by Apollo and hand him a vile of nectar. While also tasting amazing, it has slight healing properties. Great for hangovers. "That time already? They aren't going to be too thrilled about waking up so soon."

"Too bad for them. Imagine how I feel, I barely slept! I still got a job to do, though." Apollo stretches his arms and takes a swig from the vile. "Thanks, Venus."

"Anytime. Just try not to burn the world today. It would be a shame if we had to remake humanity because of a drunk driving incident." I giggle as I pick up empty bottles and throw them in the recycling bin. Yes, that's right, even goddesses recycle.

Apollo groans in frustration, "Yeah yeah, I hear you. I hate that I have to share these responsibilities with Sol. I already have enough on my plate!" He throws his hands up and shakes them angrily.

I raise my eyebrow, "Were you not the one who *asked* Jupiter for more responsibility? I distinctly remember you petitioning to be a solar deity so you can say you're 'literally hot'."

Diana, jump scaring us both, chimes in. "Yeah and somehow that got me lumped into moon duties with Luna. I wasn't even at that meeting!" Diana glances at the booth Apollo came from and snickers. "Seems like you had your fill of fun last night at least, brother. How's that hangover treating you?" She's sitting on the steps by the club entrance; up all night as usual, I imagine.

"Horribly, but I've had worse. How about you? It seems like you took my advice last night and let loose a bit." Apollo wills his clothes to change form. His half-torn and dirtied suit changes to a bright yellow Greek toga. He loves to keep it traditional.

"I did. You were right, I had fun. I still had to leave early to do my duties, but I am glad I got to enjoy myself a bit first." Diana rises from her seat.

"Good. Having fun every once in a while is good for your health. Trust me, I'm a doctor." Apollo cracks a childish grin as he walks towards the exit. "Now if you'll excuse me, I need to go wake up the people in this hemisphere."

"Yeah yeah. I need to sleep." Diana crashes into the nearest booth as her brother leaves the club.

A few moments later a burning yellow light shines through the windows of the club as the sun starts to rise. One after another everyone started waking up due to the intense brightness. Just as I predicted, not everyone is thrilled about this.

"Damnit, Apollo! Can't a war god get some rest!" Mars reaches out his arm, grabs the bottle next to him, and launches it at the skylight.

"Quiet, Mars! Some of us are still trying to sleep here!" From behind the bar, Neptune rustles around on the floor.

"My head is killing me. Stop shouting, you buffoons." Minerva mumbles under her breath.

Just as everyone is settling back in, Apollo reenters the club as loudly and obnoxiously as he can. "Wake up party people! It's daytime!" He radiates heat and a bright yellow aura. I've heard him be compared to a walking solar flare. "Rise and shine!"

"I'm going to kill him. I swear, I'm going to kill him." Jupiter sparks lightning in his fist as he rises from his seat.

"Now now, he's only doing his duties. No need to get upset at him because *you* partied too hard." Juno puts her arm around her husband's chest. "I think it is time we *ALL* got up and started our day. We have responsibilities as Olympians that we must carry out. I'm sure Venus doesn't want us loitering in her club all day like a bunch of lazy bums."

One by one the Olympians start to rise from where they drunkenly collapsed the night before. They all leave to carry out their godly duties, leaving Bacchus and I behind to clean up after the party. The gods are known for a lot of things. Cleaning their messes, however? Not one of them.

Chapter 3: Ceres Garden

I feel the sunlight on my skin as I stroll through the fields of plants. The wind blows, gently moving the bottom of my sundress. My garden is arranged by color in a rainbow-like fashion but spaced out just enough, so every plant gets its own spot to shine. Every single plant is youthful, bright, and healthy. Not a single crop or pot is out of place in my garden. Everything is perfect. Everything is how I intend it.

I bend down and examine my flowers. I find myself humming along to a song. An old song that I used to sing to my sweet Proserpina. In times like these, I miss my daughter so much. What I'd give to see her here; to see her flowing light-brown hair and her pomegranate colored dress roam my garden. I get so lost in my grief that I neglect my duties to the mortals. No crops grow, no flowers flourish; they do not deserve it. In my garden, however, I never can allow such a thing. It keeps me company in these trying times.

I look up from my roses and see a figure walking through the fields. As she approaches, I recognize who it is. A woman with her dark brunette hair braided as a crown and still wearing her white dress. Rose gold hoops hang from her ears. "You missed one amazing party last night, Ceres." Juno continues to walk towards me. She stops to pick a flower, examining its beauty.

"You know I've never been much of a party girl, Juno. I promised to be at the wedding, not the afterparty." I continue to water my plants.

"Yeah yeah, I know. Just saying it would've been nice to have you with us. Even Diana joined in." She places the flower in her hair. Why are goddesses so obsessed with that look? It kills the flower! Me personally, I like to keep my hair simple. With twisted braids, I ensure my blonde hair stays in place and out of my way. As always, though, I hide my distaste. She is queen, after all.

"Diana huh? Now that must've been a sight to see. Oh, did you get the flowers I sent for your wedding gift?" I fix the flower in her hair. If she's going to kill it, she might as well make it look nice.

"Yes, I did. They are so lovely. Thank you, you always know which ones I like. I have them in a spot right on my windowsill." Juno motions her hands in a giant square to emulate the image of a window.

"Good. I'm glad. Come on, my queen, let us walk. I have some things to take care of." I gesture for Juno to come with me as I go deeper into my garden

We continue our conversation as we stroll. The weather was perfect here. Not too cold but not too hot, with just the right amount of wind. Every type of plant flourishes in this place. I made sure of that. It's the kind of weather that, just as you start to get hot, a slight breeze blows to cool you down. It made for great walks and social gatherings as well.

Every so often, I stop to tend to the plants. As usual, this continues for hours. We talk about a variety of things; Olympian gossip, stories from the afterparty, and I give her tips on how to take care of her plants. Juno tells me about how Jupiter got so hammered, that he couldn't even tell who was who at the party anymore.

"And what of the baby? Have you thought about what kind of god or goddess it will turn out to be?" Sometimes we godly parents can have a feeling about the powers of our children. We aren't always accurate or exact, but we can usually guess the general idea.

Juno turns to me, her eyes fill with joy. "I'm not entirely sure but..." She places a hand on her stomach. "...I know it's destined for great things. The Fates have foretold that much. They say it will bring about a just world."

"Don't let Justitia hear that. You know she gets jealous about her domain." I let out a soft chuckle.

When we reach the river, my body freezes in place. I stare helplessly into the waters as they rush by. I can't tell what was wrong but I feel as if I just witnessed a murder. An intense fear surges through my body and my gut churns. Every instinct in my body says "run", yet I remain still. My limbs tremble as I fall to my knees; breathless.

"Ceres?" Juno, seeing me fall, rushes to me, "What's wrong? What happened?" She kneels in front of me and grabs my shoulders, trying to shake me out of my trance. Her voice brimming with anxiety.

I struggle to speak as my eyes slowly meet with Juno's. "I- I just sensed something...horrible. Juno, something dark. Something truly dark and terrible is coming. I haven't sensed this feeling since *the* war." My breath shakes and chills run through my spine. What did I just feel?

Chapter 4: Project Jupiter

As I sit upon my mighty throne, I look out into the skies. I can see everything from here. Every person, every alley, every sin, and every good deed. I am the god of gods, after all. Keeping up with my subjects is part of the job.

I see Neptune in his Atlantian palace, he has changed out of his suit and is now sporting his seaweed colored armor and blue undershirt. I, too, have changed from my wedding outfit. Back into something a little more comfortable; my light blue toga. Paired handsomely with my golden gauntlets, if I do say so myself.

Juno and Ceres are taking a leisurely stroll through her garden, and Apollo is sitting in his mortal apartment. I never understood why he liked to live amongst the mortals instead of with his family on the heavenly Mount Olympus. Everyone else remains performing their duties as gods.

I run my hand through my long beard. Something is wrong, I can sense it. Dark storm clouds begin to stir in the distance. Not my doing, this time. I rise from my throne, pacing impatiently around my throne room. What could this mean? I did not command these storms to form. Is one of my lords of winds starting trouble again? No. I can see them upon their own thrones. They scramble to figure out what is happening. My mind races, making me more anxious with each passing thought.

"Is there something wrong, father?" Mercury, now in his white toga with a red sash around his waist, enters the room. My son, the messenger of the gods. Maybe he can be helpful. "What's on your mind?"

"Something doesn't feel right, Mercury." My steps quicken. "I can't put my finger on what it is but something just isn't right. You know I hate not knowing what's happening."

Mercury laces up his winged sandals and grabs his brown satchel. "Shall I ask around? Maybe one of the others has noticed something."

"Yes. Go around to the other Olympians and tell them that something is coming. See if you can find out anything about what's brewing on Earth. Go." I motion for Mercury to go at once. Before I even finish lifting my hand, he's gone, moving at the speed of light. Hopefully, he will find answers for me.

"Do you think it's a war?" Mars, in an ancient greek warrior's uniform, appears from the corner of the room. He must have been listening in on the conversation. He likes to lurk around, listening in on others. He's almost as nosey as Mercury and Venus.

"I hope not. If what I'm feeling is the sign of war, it will be a big one." I walk to the edge of the mountain, looking over the Earth. Only stormy thunderclouds cross the sky.

"I could do with a good war right about now." Mars stands by my side, overlooking the mortal world. Sometimes I wonder what he sees. I wonder what all the gods see when they look at the world from this view. Do they focus on what concerns their domains? Or do they see all, as I do?

"Not one like this, Mars. There will be nothing good about this." I haven't been more concerned about war in thousands of years. If this is to be a fight, it will be the fight of our immortal lives. "I need to see Apollo. Stay here, I will be back soon."

"As you wish, father." Mars walks away and sits upon his throne. He summons his own subjects, commanding them to find answers for me.

I step over the side of the mountain. Wind flows through my long hair and mighty beard as I glide through the air. My body begins to contort and shrink, my skin morphs into feathers, a beak grows in place of my mouth, and my arms turn to wings. Transforming myself into a majestic eagle, I soar off through the storm clouds. We deities can choose any form we wish. The eagle is my bird, my symbol. A symbol of power. An apex predator.

I, in eagle form, land perched on a windowsill. Inside is a large studio apartment. It's messy but at the same time separated into sections. In one corner stands a tall booth and microphone with instruments lying around the outside of it. In another corner is the kitchen. As I continue to look, I see a desk, with many books and notepads surrounding it and, of course, a tiny two-step staircase that leads to a bed. A giant flatscreen TV is hung on the wall across from the bed. Typical mortal setups. But no mortal lives here.

Apollo is sat at his desk. He seems to be lost in whatever he is jotting down on his notepads. His short blonde hair glows in the sunlight coming through the window. If he were to ever grow facial hair, I fear it would blind us all. Occasionally, he stops writing and looks at what he's jotted down. He becomes increasingly proud of himself every time he reads his work. I sit and watch him.

Apollo starts chuckling. With his nose still dug into his notepad, he shouts, "I know you're there, dad. I can see your shadow on my wall from the sunlight." He points to the wall in front of him. Even though I am still in eagle form, my shadow still shows the figure of my godly body. He turns to face me.

"Clever as always, Apollo." I leap from the windowsill, transforming back into my normal form before my feet hit the ground.

"Well, not many eagles come sitting on my windowsill, so call it an educated guess." He pries himself from his chair and heads to the fridge.

I walk around the apartment, looking at everything. He has gained some new...trinkets... since I have been here. I pick up a random book and skim the pages. Uninterested, I throw it back to its original location. After a few minutes of looking around, I find myself in the kitchen with my son. Apollo stands, opening a bottle of water.

"Would you like a drink? Water? Maybe some nectar?" Apollo gestures towards his fridge.

"No thank you, my son. Trust me when I say I had enough nectar last night." I can't help but laugh at the suggestion. Despite my threats this morning, despite the growing darkness, I always find myself in a lighter mood around Apollo. Some people claim he is my favorite child. While I do not purposefully choose favorites, maybe there is some truth to be heard there.

"Well, then why are you here?"

His question snaps me back to reality. It's time to be serious. "I need your help. I need you to use the power of the oracle. I fear something is about to happen but I do not know what."

"It must be something serious if you need the Oracle's help. Okay, I'll try. Fair warning, I usually just give out this power to other people, I don't typically do it myself. I may be rusty." Apollo moves to the middle of his apartment where the floor is cleared and sits down crosslegged, concentrating his power.

A cold chill fills the air as Apollo's eyes start glowing green. His body lifts off the ground and the air around him starts to spiral into a ferocious wind. The voice that sounds like the cross between an old lady and a demon starts to force its way out as he speaks a prophecy. *"Soon the Olympians will hear the call. An ancient enemy rises from their fall. The rebellious children will feel their wrath. As justice prevails at last."*

Apollo falls to the ground and the wind stops abruptly. The warmth from the sunlight reenters the room. The apartment is torn apart. Blood oozes from Apollo's nose. "No, don't worry, dad. I'm fine. I can get up myself." As he stands and jokes, he looks in my direction. I guess I wasn't too good at hiding my true emotions. Hiding my *fear*. "What? What did the prophecy say?"

"This is impossible. If it means what I think it means, we are all in grave danger." I hurry back to the windowsill.

"Grave danger? We are gods, what can put us in grave danger?" Apollo stops me. We look out over the city.

"There were gods long before us, my son. I need you to find your sister and get to Olympus.

Immediately." I wave my hand out the window, motioning Apollo to leave with haste.

"Gods before us? What do you..." I watch as his look of confusion turns to understanding. "I need to find Diana." Apollo summons his golden chariot to the window. He jumps out of his apartment and into the chariot, flying off. I hope we can stop this in time. My worst fears are becoming true.

I turn myself into an eagle. With as much speed as I can muster, I head back to Olympus. I land on the mountainside and rush towards the throne room. "Mars! Mars where are you!' I shout as I storm into the throne room.

"What is it, father? Did you speak with Apollo?" Mars jolts up from his throne to meet up with me at the entrance.

I don't stop walking, talking to Mars as I go. "Yes, I did. It's far worse than I feared. The prophecy said '*Soon the Olympians will hear the call. An ancient enemy rises from their fall. The rebellious children will feel their wrath. As justice prevails at last.*' If it means what I think it does, we need to prepare. Send a message to Mercury." I hurry to our war room, shouting my orders behind me.

"Prepare for what, father?! What does it mean?! What message?!" Mars yells after me as he tries to keep up with my pace.

"You are going to get your war, Mars. If the prophecy means what I think... then the Titans are rising once more." For the first time in almost a millennium, I ring the great bell. The bell that summons all gods and goddesses back to Olympus. As the bell chimes, my subject will understand its message; *war*.

Chapter 5: Halls of Atlantis

The palace trembles. After the ceiling in the throne room collapsed, I sent all of my subjects to take refuge in the depths of the sea. I pace my long and twisting hallways, trying to figure out what is going on. It's taking all of my power to keep the waters from destroying my palace completely. Whatever is causing this, *whoever* is causing this, must wield immense power. Could it be...

Mercury bursts into the hallway. A gush of wind slaps my face, I hate it when he does that. "Neptune, what's going on? It's like your entire kingdom is crumbling down!"

"Well that's the question of the hour, nephew. I feel my control over the seas slipping. It's

as if it's fighting back. Every time I pull, it pushes."
I summon my mighty trident. The weapon glows
gold as I tighten my grip around it. I feel my power
resonating through the cold metal.

"What are you going to do with that?"
Mercury follows me down the halls. I designed the
walls of my hallway to be made of glass, making the
outside perfectly visible. The ocean life swims all
around us. They're moving around the palace
unusually. Sharks are swimming alongside their
prey, circling us. Something is happening out there.

"As you know, my trident helps amplify my
control over the seas. I will use its power and mine
to try and calm the water. Wait here, Mercury." I
open the door and hurry outside. It's a good thing
my barrier is still intact, or Mercury would've been
hit with the full weight of the seas. On second
thought, I would love to see that.

I make my way to the top of the palace. With
my trident in my hands, I raise my arms as high as I

can and slam it down into the roof. A wave of energy ripples through the water, pushing all the sealife back away from the palace. For a moment, this seems to have worked. The seas calmed and the creatures of my realm swam away.

I feel a massive pulse in the current as the sea violently pushes back. Sealife ignores my commands as much as the water. A huge wave smacks me in the face, blowing me off the roof. My weapon falls from my grasp. I must head back inside. Making a quick burst for the trident, I grab it and swim back to the door. I need to tell Mercury. This is worse than I thought.

"What the Hades was that? Why were they ignoring you? Why did the sea just lash back out? You're supposed to be the sea god! This is *your* domain!" Mercury screams at me but, in his eyes, I sense fear rather than anger. I can't blame the young god.

Mercury follows me down the halls with haste. We must get to my portal room. It's the quickest way to get to Olympus. "I do not know for sure but there's only one reason something like that could ever happen..."

"Well? What is the reason?" Mercury keeps close behind.

Before I answer him, I need to confirm my theory. Jupiter must have sent his messenger for a reason. "Why are you here, nephew? You never come here unless my brother sends a message. What was so important that Jupiter needed to send you?"

"Father said that he felt a disturbance. He doesn't know what it was for sure but he wants me to warn the Olympians. He fears something is coming, something big. He also wanted me to try and find out more info on this hidden enemy. Do you think this has something to do with that?" Mercury and I now stand face to face. I see his concern growing, as does mine. If Jupiter felt that big of a disturbance, then my theory must be correct.

"Yes, I do. The only thing that could turn the seas against me was the Titan Oceanus. This palace used to be his. The sea around here has always tried to resist my control. The only way it'd be able to resist me fully is if its original master has awoken." I look out the windows, and my concern morphs to horror as I ponder the possibilities. My brother is right, this is not a good sign.

Mercury tries to laugh it off, but I hear the nervousness in his words. "Are you saying you think the Titans are waking? Don't be ridiculous, uncle. They are locked in Tartarus! How could Oceanus be thwarting you?" Normally, he'd be correct. However, Oceanus was neutral during the first war, so we let him remain topside. I fear his neutrality has wavered.

Suddenly, the ringing of a loud bell fills my ears. Mercury covers his ears as we both look towards the skies. We can't see it, of course, but we know that sound. The war bell on Olympus has been rung. I only hope we aren't too late to stop this. I head over to my portal. "I need you to go to Tartarus and check out what's going on down there. Be fast, the war bell of Olympus is calling us. I will let my brother know where I sent you. Go, see what is happening down there, warn Pluto, and meet me on Olympus with your report."

"Yes, of course." Mercury takes off towards the underworld without hesitation.

Going through my portal, I make my way to Olympus. Upon my arrival, I head to the war room. I assume most of the Olympians have arrived already. When I breach through the doorway I notice that everyone minus Pluto, Proserpina and, of course, Mercury have beat me here. Diana, Vulcan, and Venus all look confused as to why they were summoned. The rest, however, clearly have experienced similar troubles as I have. One thing is for certain, we all are worried.

Everyone is back in their normal attire. Vulcan is back in his dirty apron, jeans and brown boots. Minerva wears a bronze breastplate over her white clothing, her emerald gauntles now back on her wrists. Diana looks as if she's been hunting in the woods again, her cammo outfit filled with grass stains. Speaking of stains, Bacchus has returned to his wine-stained green and purple casual wear.

"By the look on your faces, I assume most of you are aware of the current situation." I take one last glance around the room.

Jupiter speaks from the head of the table. "Yes, brother. I fear the worst. What of Mercury? Last I checked he was with you in Atlantis."

"After Atlantis started crumbling, I tried to use my powers over the seas to stop it. However, the ocean started resisting me more than it ever had before. It fought back, my brother." I force that last remark out through gritted teeth. "I quickly realized only Oceanus could be doing this, only he has that kind of power over my domain. So I sent Mercury to the underworld on a scout mission. I told him to report here on any Titan activity in Tartarus and to warn Pluto of the events." I take my place next to Jupiter and Juno.

"I see, wise decision to send him." Jupiter stroks his beard. It looks grayer than usual. His face is more aged.

Venus frantically looks around the table. "Wait...Oceanus? Titans? Is that what this is about?"

"That would explain why the volcanic forge has been restless." Vulcan places his chin in his rough hands.

"This is bad indeed if it is true. From the stories, the last war against the Titans was barely won. We may have more gods now, but I still don't like the sound of this." Minerva studies the map of Earth that sits on the table in front of her.

"I share the sentiment, Minerva. That is why I called you all here today. We must come up with a strategy in case our fears are realized. We must prepare ourselves for the worst." Jupiter rises from his chair. "This will be our most difficult task as gods."

I place my hands on the table in front of me. "We will need to combine all our strength. Even Pluto. I just hope Mercury gets the message to him in time..."

Chapter 6: Dark Magic

I look upon my scales once more, nothing has changed. A few days ago, they shifted out of balance. I can not allow this to remain. I need to consort with the Oracle. Sitting upon my throne, I focus my energies within myself. Apollo isn't the only deity who has personal access to such prophetic powers.

The air swirls around me and a small breeze hits my skin. A green aura traces my body as I begin to speak. *"Soon the Olympians will hear the call. An ancient enemy rises from their fall. The rebellious children will feel their wrath. As justice prevails at last."* Interesting. As I ponder the words of prophecy, images begin to invade my mind. A child born with immense power, the world in a state of destruction, my scales broken at my feet as I lay in a fiery wasteland.

In the vision, my normally neatly done bun of black hair has unravelled, making me look almost feral. My brown dress is wrinkled and messy. Not to mention, the orange hue in my skin seems to have faded, turning me to a pale lifeless husk. The hazel coloring of my eyes are completely gone.

What does this all mean? Who was that child? Why were my scales broken? Who could have defeated me if justice is to prevail? I am Justitia, goddess of justice! In my rage, a small explosion of divine energy bursts around me, destroying my throne. I look at my scales once more, pondering these questions.

An immense feeling of realization dawns on me. My eyes widen as I piece together the puzzle. I remember hearing something earlier in the day. A piece of conversation between Juno and Ceres. I never eavesdrop on the queen of Olympus but I heard my power be invoked. She had said "The

Fates have foretold that much. They say it will bring about a just world." The Fates...the child....a just world. I shout a rageful scream as everything clicks into place. They want to replace me!

I knew Juno secretly disliked me. I am Jupiter's ex-wife, after all. Together we sired many children. But I could never imagine they would do this to me.

Voices rush through my mind, whispering my worst fears. "Betrayal," one says. "Unjust," another speaks. "They could never really trust a Titan" the final comment breaks me. My vision goes blurry as tears fill my eyes. Anger surges through my veins. I am the goddess of justice and I have been severely wronged. I know of others who feel the same. Scorned and cast aside by Jupiter and his Olympians. It is time I do what I should have done years ago. It's time for me to visit *that* place.

I'll use my magic to travel through the air. I would use the portal on Olympus, but I don't wish to be tracked. My molecules split as my body became air. Using the currents of the winds I aim for the entrance to the realm of Hades.

As I enter, the light from the sun disappears. All that is left is darkness, the only light being the green flames lining the walls. The waters of the Styx below me glow a teal color. I see Charon, the ferryman of souls, riding his boat, flowing with the currents. I stay high above the river so he does not spot me. I must go deeper.

I pass through the Fields of Asphodel, where mortal souls wander for eternity. This is just one of many fields in Hades, of course. As I fly through his realm, I ensure I do not go near Pluto's castle. It's likely he's sensed my presence already, I can feel eyes watching me from afar. But I knew that risk when I came here. I must not draw his attention further, for I fear he will stop me.

Up ahead of me, I can finally see the light. Not the light of the sun, mind you, but the orange hue of this damned place. A place where even the mighty Olympians fear to go. A place full of the world's most evil creatures; monsters, giants, and most importantly, Titans. I feel the hot air against my skin as I land on a rocky mountainside. I am here. I have entered... *Tartarus*.

Chapter 7: Speed of Mercury

Energy pumps through my legs as I make my way to Hades. Wind rips my skin, and my goggles protect my eyes, allowing me to see as I fly through the air. Many mortals depict me as either running or flying, but the truth is, I do both. My winged shoes allow me to hover in the air as I use the force from my legs to zip through the skies. I'm so awesome.

I enter the realm of Hades. Dark caverns twist and turn under the earth, lit only by the green hue of the Greek flames. I see my uncle's palace in the distance. I must....wait a minute. I feel another presence in the air, someone with a dark energy. Unable to see the intruder, I follow the presence I feel. Who is this mysterious being? Why are they sneaking around the Underworld?

 I keep my distance as we fly above the Fields of Asphodel. Where are they heading? It's not to Pluto's palace. Why do they feel the need to conceal themselves from my uncle's sight? I must find out these answers before I bring the news to Pluto. I have a feeling this is important.

 We fly farther down into the depths. I begin to see an orange light casting a shadow on the walls. No...it can't be. This is the entrance to Tartarus! Not even my father, Jupiter, dares visit this place. What business does this being have here? Who would....

 As my mind races, the mysterious energy reveals itself. Or should I say, *herself.* Her molecules recombine as she takes form once again. I would recognize her anywhere. But what is Justitia doing in Tartarus? Surely she should be on

Olympus advising my father. Whatever this is, it can't be good.

I keep myself concealed as I continue my search for answers. Following just far enough behind her, I struggle to find the reasoning behind her visit. What could Justitia possibly need in Tartarus? As we round the corner of this mountain, I find my answers. She's come to see her siblings.

"Ah, sister, you have come at last." A deep and raspy voice spoke. A giant being made of molten rock sits chained and bound to the mountain behind him. Each of his horns are longer than my forearm and fire rages in his eyes.

Justitia cautiously keeps her distance as she answers him. "You knew I was coming, Saturn? Do tell." I detect a hint of disdain in her voice.

Saturn speaks once more. "Yes, my sister, I knew of your visit. You see, as I sit bound to this mountain, I can not move. I can not eat or drink. I can not ever feel the sunlight on my skin. But I am still the lord of time. I can see glimpses into the future. Nothing close to the power of your Oracle, mind you, but I see enough. I knew of your arrival before you even knew you were coming here." His voice is cracked and scratchy. Not being able to drink for millions of years will do that to a guy, I suppose.

"Does that mean...did you see my prophecies too? Do you know what the visions mean?" Justitia steps closer to the rotting Titan. I've never heard her speak like this. So frantic and scared, she searches for answers as big as I do.

"I do not pretend to know for certain, but I do have an idea of what they mean. I believe you have also come to the same conclusions as I." Saturn's tone sounds almost triumphant. What is his game here? The lord of time can't be trusted. "They plan to replace you, Justitia. To throw you to the side like they did to me and your other siblings.

Cast you into damnation. The Olympians are a traitorous brood."

What is he talking about? Juno and my father would never betray her. They value her advice and power too much. We all do. I want to speak out but I can't afford to get caught here. For now, I need to wait and listen. Don't fall for his lies, Justitia.

"If what you speak is true, then I have no other options. If the Olympians plan to turn on me, then I must strike first." She moves towards the locks that hold Saturn's chains together. "I will bring justice to my fallen brothers and sisters!" She cuts the king of the Titans loose.

I can't hold my silence. "No!" I shout from behind the rocks. Good job, Mercury, you just gave away your position.

Justitia whips her head in my direction. Her nostrils flare as she looks at me with rage. It's official, she's lost it. "I knew someone was spying on me! I assumed it was Pluto sensing me enter his realm, but it was you this whole time wasn't it, Mercury?" She lifts her hand in my direction. What is she about to do?

As I ready myself to dodge whatever attack she is about to hurl my way, Saturn stands up. He towers over us both, almost as tall as the mountain he was chained to. "No, Justitia, let the little godling go. It matters not if he warns the others now that I am free. Come, let us free the rest of our family." Saturn turns and walks away. Justitia lowers her hand and follows.

They just...let me go? Why? Am I not important enough for the lord of time? I shake my head, trying to grasp reality. These questions are not important. My mission is. I must warn Pluto and the Olympians.

Chapter 8: Pluto's Den

"Hmmm," Walking through my throne room, I pace in circles. My heavy boots thud against the concrete floors with each step. The bottom of my black jacket flaps in the hot winds.

"What is wrong, husband?" Proserpina, my beautiful wife, remains sat upon her throne. Unlike mine, this chair is not her seat of power. Hers remains on Olympus with the other gods. Nonetheless, for six months of the year, this acts as her throne. The reds and purples on her dress blend together, making a pomegranate-like color. Her dress almost matches the red of my shirt. She brings a goblet to her lips, most likely filled with nectar.

I turn to face her, flicking back my long black hair. She lays across her throne as if everything is normal. She does not sense what I do. "Something is stirring. I can feel it but can't pinpoint where this disturbance is coming from." My pacing quickens as my hands rustle through my french-forked beard.

Out of nowhere, the doors leading to the throne room burst open with a gust of wind. The heavy golden doors fall off their hinges, crashing to the ground. Standing there, in the center of the destruction, is Mercury.

He inhales a shaky breath before speaking my worst fears, "Titans, uncle! The Titans are returning!" He collapses to his knees. His face is as pale as mine. Whatever he saw must have been terrible.

"What?!" Proserpina shouts from her throne. She rises with haste. "Did he just say *Titans*? Impossible!"

I help up my fallen nephew. "I say, I must agree with my wife, young nephew. Explain yourself." I stand him up against the wall, giving him a place to lean. "Why have you destroyed my entrance? I thought you had control of your powers of speed. Could you not have at least slowed down?" I point to the destruction he caused. "And what is this Titian business you speak of? They are locked away in Tartarus."

Through shallowed breaths, Mercury begins his tale, "Earlier this morning, father sent me to warn all the gods. He believed something big was coming, and he was right. After I spoke with Neptune, father rang the bells. Did you not hear them ring?" He glances between my wife and I.

"Yeah, we heard it. Didn't care. My brother can fight a war without my assistance. I figured it was a trivial squabble he overreacted to again." I shrug. It was true that the war bell hasn't been rung in centuries, but it's also true we gods can be petty.

Mercury grabs my shoulders, gripping tightly. "Listen to me, uncle! It was not a false alarm! As I came here to warn you, I noticed a presence in your realm. I followed the energy I felt and it was Justitia!" His speech becomes more frantic as he talks.

"And, pray tell, what was the goddess of justice doing in my husband's realm?" She eyes me up and down. Is this something I'm going to have to hear about later? I can't help but let out a stressed sigh.

"I followed her down to Tartarus. While spying on her, I found out her intent. She went to speak with **Saturn**. She *freed* him." His attention flicks between us. "Pluto...Proserpina...she's going to free them all!"

Proserpina gasps. The goblet she holds shatters against the concrete floor, spilling her drink everywhere. "That's what the bells meant. Husband, we must go to Olympus immediately!"

The ground beneath us begins to shake and tremble. "They are coming," I whisper, staring out the windows of my throne room. I see mountains in the distance being destroyed and tall creatures plowing through the fields. Hades no longer holds power over the Titans.

Mercury heads in the direction of my portal room. "Come, uncle, we must leave-"

"No. You two must go without me." I summon my helm of darkness and mighty bident to me.

Mercury halts in his place. Is that, shock on his face? Concern? "But, uncle, all the Olympians must stand together if we are to win this war." The ground continues to tremble beneath us. In the distance, I can hear the palace guards fighting. No. *Dying.*

My blood begins to boil. *All the Olympians.* I shout, "I am no Olympian, nephew. I am Pluto, lord of the dead and ruler of the Underworld. Vesta may have given me her seat, but I can never be one of you. Not really. My duties down here are too important."

My darling wife runs to me. I squeeze her tight in what feels like our final embrace. We weren't the most perfect couple, the Fates know I've done some awful things, but I love her. "Be careful, Pluto." She runs off and enters the portal.

"What will you do, uncle?" Mercury shouts one final question.

Letting out a guttural scream, I slam my bident into the ground. The metal skull on my belt buckle presses against my stomach as I bend. A crack in the floor appears between us and continues to widen. Skeletal and zombified warriors climb up through the cracks. I summon all I can muster. I turn my head back to Mercury, unable to help cracking a smile. "You go do your job, messenger god. And I shall do mine." I swipe my bident through the air with enough force to cause a small bit of wind to send Mercury flying through the portal.

Chapter 9: Mind of Minerva

As the rest of the Olympians speak, I remain silent. I remain calm. As the goddess of wisdom and war, it is imperative that I keep my cool during these stressful times. I fear what father says is true. Mars and I can feel when a war is brewing, and the timer is almost up.

"What do we do? How can we prepare for war?" Bacchus chimes in. This is the first time in millennia that I've seen him without a drink in his hand. Even the foolish can sense their impending doom.

"What say you, Minerva, you are the smartest thing to come from dad's head, after all." Apollo, always the jester.

"Watch it, Apollo. This is no time for jokes!" Jupiter slams his mighty hand on the table. The noise from the impact is enough to make us all straighten up. Except Apollo, who slumps back into his throne, trying to escape into the back of it.

"Well," I finally speak my piece. "In order to make a plan, we need to know *exactly* what we are dealing with here. Neptune," I turn to my rival. "You said that we were being attacked by Oceanus. Is there any possibility it was someone else? Did you actually *see* the Titan?" I pray to the Fates that he could have been mistaken.

Neptune stares intensely at the table with his chin in his hands. "I did not physically see him, no. But I'm sorry, Minerva, it was definitely Oceanus. Only he could have pushed against me like that. I know it." The certainty in his voice is unmistakable. He looks at no one, only the table. A fierce dance of fear and rage gleems in his eyes.

"But the Titans are locked away in Tartarus, how could-" Venus is quickly cut off by the loud sounds of metal scraping. The doors to the war room open.

Stepping through the doorway, Mercury and Proserpina arrive. "Daughter!" Ceres jumps from her throne and sprints towards Prosperina. She embraces her daughter in a tight squeeze, but Prosperina just stands there; distraught. Her knuckles whiten as she tightens her grip on her black dagger. Something had happened in the Hades.

"What is it? What's wrong, Proserpina? Tell us what happened," As I speak, Ceres lets go of her daughter and notices her daughter's demeanor. Quickly, I surmise that I will get no answers from Proserpina in her current state. So I turn my attention to Mercury. I didn't notice before, but he seems equally down in spirit. "Mercury, explain."

The two goddesses make their way to their thrones and take their spots at the table. Mercury, however, walks to the head of the table. No one ever approaches father's spot without permission, but Mercury seems to not care.

"Father," he begins to speak, "gods and goddesses of Olympus. We have been betrayed. Pluto is gone." He looks solemnly at the ground. Proserpina starts weeping. His words must be true. A collective gasp can be heard all around the table as we look to one another, hoping for answers.

Father's eyes fill with electricity. His anger can be felt in the air. "What is the meaning of this? Hurry and explain yourself, son."

Mercury addresses the table. "As I'm sure you all know by now, after I visited Neptune in Atlantis, he sent me off to Hades in order to inform Pluto and Proserpina of the current situation." The deities grumble in agreement. "Well, as I entered Pluto's realm I felt a disturbing presence. I tasked myself with finding the source. As I followed the energy I discovered it was Justitia who I felt. I followed her to Tartarus, where she met with Saturn himself."

"What?!" Juno roars in outrage. "Why would the goddess of justice meet with that vile being?!"

"She was jealous," Mercury turns to Juno, pointing to her stomach, "Jealous that this child would somehow take her place. I don't know how she came to that conclusion, but it's true." Juno rushes to father's arms. "She freed the Titan king right before I made my escape. I immediately sought out Pluto and Proserpina in their palace." He gestures to a crying Proserpina. "While we spoke, however, the Titans began escaping Tartarus."

Father finally responds. "And what of my brother? Where is Pluto now?" He asks, but we all know the answer.

"He stayed behind to fight on his own. He sacrificed himself so I could get you this information, father. I'm sorry." After his revelations, Mercury goes back to his own throne, sitting down defeated.

The silence is loud and brutal. I look at Pluto's empty throne. It was not long ago when he wasn't even accepted up here with us. The Olympians and Pluto have always had a complicated history. That is until Vesta decided to give up her seat in hopes of healing that rift. But now those hopes are over. It is true that we gods cannot die, but it is also true that there are fates worse than death.

I break the silence. "Well then, we now know who are enemy is." One by one they all look to me. I need to make a plan. "First thing's first, Vulcan, I need you to make as much magical armor as you can. They need to be the strongest you have ever created. We will also need weapons. Powerful ones."

"But, Minerva, these are Titans. I don't know if I can-"

"You will do this, Vulcan. You *must*. Mars and I will think of a battle strategy. Diana, call any of your followers that can fight. As a matter of fact," I look out to all the deities in this meeting, "Call all of your servants and warriors. We must all fight if we hope to survive. Olympus barely won last time, but we will do it again."

Just like that, the Olympians spring into action. This leaves only Mars, Juno, father, and myself in the war room. We must come up with a strategy to stop the coming threat. If we don't succeed, the world as we know it will be lost.

Chapter 10: Forge in the Flames

Sweat drips from my brow as I hammer the golden armor in front of me. I need more time to create what is possibly my most important pieces of work. Time I do not have. The cyclopes under my command work diligently in the forge, following my every order to the most minute details. While their one eye may seem like a disability, they far make up for it in strength and a knowledge of forgery embedded deep within their genetics. We must not fail. We *will* not.

I built my forge deep in the heart of a volcano, using the heat that radiates off the magma to smelt whatever metals I required. You may wonder how someone can live inside an active volcano. The answer is simple, I am the god of forges. I am Vulcan, the master craftsman of Olympus. Despite my complaining to annoy my wife, I can take the heat. Even so, doubt creeps into my mind. Will my skills be enough? I didn't fight in the last war, it was before my time. I can only hope I pass this ultimate test.

While I craft this breastplate, I have my servants working on the weaponry. These weapons are important, but I believe we will need all the defensive power we can muster. The creators of the greatest weapons, dad's master bolt, Poseidon's trident, and Pluto's helm of darkness, were all cyclopes. While the original creators have perished, thanks to Apollo, I can only hope that their descendants can create weaponry of equal value.

If what Mercury says is true, the Titan armies will be upon us within a matter of hours. Minerva and Mars better come up with a good strategy, or else my crafts will mean nothing. I've never been to Tartarus myself, never even looked upon the face of a Titan, but I've heard the stories.

Beings that tower over mountains. Beings with immense strength and incredible powers. I think back to my war with the Giants as a reference for the coming battle.

I land the final strike on the enchanted armor. I received help from a few friends, friends of other worlds, and practices. They aid with the magic embedded in the armor. Spells of durability, strange symbols from far lands that grant the wearer strength, and small healing ability. These enchantments will bless every piece that comes out of this forge today. We shall be as prepared for this war as we can. Though the armor looks basic, these will hopefully bring us luck in battle.

Clumsy, loud footsteps approach behind me. It's the leader of the cyclopes forge, "What is it? Aren't you supposed to be crafting weapons? We don't have much time here!" I can't even spare a glance in his direction, I must start the next piece.

"Sir, while we were working in the forge, looking through thousands of pages worth of notes left by our predecessors, we found something that may be of use." The cyclops leader babbles on, eager to show me his revelations. "We found the blueprints to another weapon the Master Cyclopes never got to build. A weapon to rival that of Jupiter's master bolt."

My hammer falls from my grasp. I turn to the cyclops. "What?! A weapon to rival the bolt? What is it!? Let me see this weapon immediately!"

"Well, it's not a weapon per se..." The cyclops hands me the blueprints.

I open the scroll with haste. What the Hades is this? "A crown? You came to me about a *CROWN*?! We are fighting a war! Not throwing a beauty pageant. This is better suited for my wife. *After* this war." I throw the scroll back at him. Bending down, I reach and grab my hammer from the ground.

"You don't understand, sir. This isn't just any crown. It's a crown meant for the queen of the heavens. A crown of protection."

I stop once more, "A crown of protection? That does sound intriguing. Explain."

"It is said, if made correctly, the crown radiates an immense aura of healing and protection for anyone the wearer wishes. It's the ultimate defense to the bolt's offense." The cyclops looks squeamish as I turn to him again.

"Well then, this could be useful. Mom would love something like this." I ponder the uses of the crown, "Alright, do whatever you can to make sure this crown is completed to every detail!"

The cyclops can't look at me, his eye is locked on the floor and his hands fiddle with the buttons on his shirt. "There's one issue, sir. I don't know if we will be able to craft it in time. Even the

Master Cyclopes never completed their prototype in time."

    This is not the answer I'm looking for. "Well, we better hope that you and your forges can do better, for all our sakes." I wave him off to start his task as I finish the assignments I already have.

Chapter 11: Sirens of War

Power surges through me as I strap the golden armor to my body. Vulcan has outdone himself this time. My comrades stand beside me as we brace for battle. The fields below Mount Olympus are barren, with no animal life in sight. Even they can sense what's coming.

I feel a hand place itself on my shoulder. "The plan will work, Mars. It *has* to work." Minerva and I always fought over the domain of war, but today I'm glad we are on the same page. We may have our differences, and our own way of battle, but when crunch time comes, we can make quite the team.

The plan. During our war council on Olympus, Minerva and I had devised a 3 step strategy. Step 1) Father, Bacchus, Venus, Apollo, and I will make our stand here at the base of the mountain while Minerva remains on the high ground, where she can see the battle and strategize further. Step 2) Neptune guards the oceanfront while Diana, Mother, Ceres, and Proserpina flank through the woods surrounding the battlefield. A classic pinch move. Step 3) Hold out long enough for Vulcan and his cyclopes to create that crown. If we can win without it, even better.

During all this, Mercury will act as our messenger. Carrying orders from Minerva to our troops and gathering as much intel as possible during the fight. All while simultaneously using his speed to knock down any of the fodder in his way. They'll never see what hit them.

The Titans will no doubt bring armies of their own. Monsters, forgotten deities, and maybe even the Giants. But we Olympians are not without our armies. Behind us stand rows upon rows of battle-ready satyrs, cyclopes, Diana's followers, and creatures so rare even I forget their names. War is coming but we are prepared. As ready as we can be, anyway.

So why do nerves course through my body as much as confidence does? Why do I feel as if we are only prolonging our demise? "Father," I turn to the god of gods. He remains staring out over the fields, unwavering. "Do you think we can win?"

"Mars, my son, I have the two best war gods commanding our armies. There are no doubts in my mind about the coming battle." He never loses his focus. Warm words from my father? This definitely is wrong.

The ground begins to quake beneath us. They're here. Giant figures with monstrous faces appear over the tree lines. I slam my spear into the ground, steeling my nerves. I am the god of war. I will not fall here.

"Get ready, soldiers! Here comes our prey!" With renewed confidence, I prepare my armies.

They form ranks behind us. To my left, Bacchus and Venus stand tall. To my right, father and Apollo ready their weapons. Part of me is glad Venus is here by my side. Another part of me wishes she had stayed back with Minerva.

The trees crumble beneath the feet of the Titans. Hordes of monsters flood the battlefield. Empussa, vampiric like creatures with snakes for legs, and enemy cyclopes stand with the evil Titans. I think I even spot a few manticore. Excellent.

"Ready?!" I scream to my soldiers. Apollo knocks an arrow in his bow as our father rises to the skies, electricity radiating off his body. "Charge!"

The moment I give the command, we rush into battle. Apollo's arrows ring true as they take out one monster after another. Bacchus tries to slow the Titans with vines tied around their legs.

Venus uses her powers of persuasion to turn enemies on their comrades. Father rains lightning from the heavens, striking dozens at a time.

With all my might, I chuck my spear, and shish kabob 3 cyclopes at once. Lunging forward, my hands grip around the base of my weapon as I remove it from their skulls. I hack and slash my way through the enemy line with blinding fury. There are more uses for a spear than just projectiles.

"Mars!" Apollo shouts from the mountainside, launching an arrow into the throat of an empusa trying to sneak behind me. "Gotta be more careful than that, half-brother!" I can sense his smug look from way out here. That guy pisses me off sometimes.

Bacchus runs to my side. "I have an idea. Follow my lead." He disappears into the ground as quickly as he came. Since when does he have ideas?

In front of me, I spot my target. The red Titan Atlas was the closest thing the Titans had to a war deity. His bulging muscles may scare most, but not me. However, I can't help but wonder two very important questions: How did they free him from his prison? Who holds the Earth now that Atlas abandoned his post? There's only one way to find out. With a fierce scream, I charge my opponent.

Atlas remains distracted as Bacchus, appearing from the dirt behind him, uses his vines to wrap around the Titan's legs like tendrils. I use my spear to slash at his ankles. Thanks for leaving part of it exposed, Bacchus. The Titan roars in pain as silver blood pours from his wounds.

"Tiny godlings. I will decimate you!" His voice is full of bass and rage. His dark black eyes search the battlefield for his attackers.

With Bacchus's help, this will be a piece of cake. "I'd like to see you try!" All my previous doubts are replaced by renewed confidence as I face my opponent.

The universe loves to correct me. I go to launch another attack but a giant fist the size of a building swats me like a fly. As I soar through the air, I catch my grip on a tree branch. Using the inertia built up from that hit, the branch bends before cracking like a whip and sending me hurling back at the Titan.

"Nice try, but you'll have to do worse than that to stop me!" The branch gave me enough height to sink my spear into his abdomen. Using my free hand, I latch onto his course and rough skin. "Now die!"

Chapter 12: The Hunt

Knocking an arrow in my bow, I line my shot. Once my enemy enters my sight, I fire. An enemy empusa drops to the ground, while her squad quickly searches the woods. But they can not find me. They are nothing but prey, and I am the predator. This is my hunt.

Ceres and Proserpina latch vines onto the other 2 empusa, holding them in place. Juno jumps from a neighboring bush, her knife in hand. She slashes the enemy's throats before they have any time to react.

"Nice work," I keep my voice low so as to not alert other enemies. "Now get back into position, everyone. There are surely more to come." Just like that, we vanish.

We continue our ambush method of attack on the next few squads that come through. In order to not blow our cover, we hide the bodies in whatever bush is closest. After our last attack, the ground begins to shake. The big ones are coming.

"Everyone, hide," Ceres whispers, covering us with shrubbery so we blend into the forest.

Her disguise works. The Titans walk right by us, not noticing a thing. They crush trees beneath them as they march to Olympus. Only 2 of them, though. The others can't be too far behind. No way any of them would want to miss this fight.

The sound of lightning cracks through the air as the fight begins. From the forest, the battle cries of both armies can be heard. The ground trembles and leaves fall from destroyed and quaking trees. All we can do is play our part and hope the others survive.

I wish I had my followers with me, but they are needed elsewhere. Juno, Ceres, Proserpina, and I stay in the bushes, waiting for our prey to enter the trap. Yes, there are already armies of monsters and a few Titans fighting, but the rest are nowhere to be seen. Where are they? No Saturn, no Japetus, not even Justistia has shown her traitorous face. Just Atlas and Hyperion. This strategy will only work once, if we expose ourselves now, we may not get another shot.

Nearby, ocean waves crash and collide, and storms brew on the surface of the water. Oceanus is here too, it seems. Neptune is holding him off for now. Suddenly, a figure gets thrown into the trees. Is that Mars? He grabs the thickest branch in his way and sling-shots himself back into battle. Say what you want about my half-brother, but he has gusto.

"It looks like the rest aren't coming, Diana." Juno breaks our silence.

Looking back on where the two Titans came from, there are no signs of a second invasion force. "I fear you may be right, my queen."

"What should we do? If we help now, our cover will be blown. If we stay and wait, we risk the others falling without our aid." Proserpina speaks true. We must make a decision now.

"You're in charge of this unit, Diana, what is your call?" Ceres looks at me, her eyes full of power and determination.

"Screw it, let's send these bastards back where they came from!" We charge from our posts, entering the field of combat.

The treeline clears as a landscape of blood and death fills our vision. Monsters and satyrs slain all the same. Mercury zooms through the battle, picking off the stragglers of monsters that are left. We may be able to win this battle after all.

A bloodied and scarred Bacchus approaches us. "Please tell me you're here because you beat the rest on your own."

"Not quite, where's Mercury?" Juno wastes no time in calling over the messenger god.

His heels dig two deep lines into the dirt as he makes his stop. "Right here. What's the news?" I've never heard him so out of breath. He's been using his powers of speed all day, way before this battle even began. I'm quite shocked he's still standing.

"The other Titans aren't coming. Other than Oceanus fighting Neptune in the water, we see no more signs of enemies. We've decided to join in the fight now and end this. Go, tell dad." He was gone before I even finished the final sentence.

Bacchus's eyes widen before he lets out a long sigh. "Well, I hoped this would be all over soon so I could have a stiff drink, but I guess this war will be prolonged some more. For now, let's give these ugly scumbags a fight to remember, eh?"

Mars lands on the ground in front of us, causing a crater to appear. "What's with all this yapping!? Bacchus, he got free because you stopped paying attention!" He rose from the crater, fixing his chest plate as he stood. His face was cut and bruised, his armor had dents and pieces broken clean off. So much for those protection enchantments. Then, he snaps himself back into battle mode. "Ceres, Proserpina, Bacchus, you three stay by the treelines and use your woodland magics and earth magics to help keep these bastards standing in place. Mother, I'm sure father would rather you by his side. Diana, help your brother with our cover fire. Rain down as many arrows as you two possibly can. Go!"

Just like that, we all spring into action. Moving as fast as I can, I run to Apollo's side. "Miss me, little brother?" A smile creeps its way onto my face as I see him virtually unharmed.

"We're twins! You're barely older than me!" He protests.

"I'm older by a day," I grin.

Apollo drops his bow and turns to me, "You know, sometimes I think you just made that up!" He flails his arms like a child, I love riling him up like this. "It just makes absolutely no sense!" He calms himself, changing his tone. I can sense a hint of relief in his voice. "But, yes, I was a little bit worried." Normally, he would never admit such a thing. Neither of us would.

Apollo grabs his bow and resumes his post. Arrows cover the skies as we rapidly fire on our enemies. The two deities of archery, side by side, I feel an incredible surge of strength and skill just by standing next to him. By the looks of it, it was the same for him.

While we fire, I scan the battlefield, searching for my followers. "No..." I can barely make out the word. My followers...my friends, brave souls they were, are dead. Some were pinned to trees by spears and horns of monsters. Others lay flattened on the ground, in craters shaped like a Titan's footprint. Cold tears trace my face.

"I'm sorry, dear sister. I could not save them..." It's as if he could read my thoughts. I turn to him. Is he...crying too? A small teardrop rushes down his cheek. "I know how much they meant to you."

Seeing Apollo grieve with me made it all too real. Steeling my nerves, my attack becomes even more relentless. My rage adds fuel to the fires burning inside me, as my arrows sink into Hyperion's thick golden skin. I will avenge you, my brothers and sisters in arms. I will defeat this foe in your honor. I swear it!

Chapter 13: Olympians Fall

Commanding the vines of the forest, I trap Hyperion's right leg in place once again. His lean muscles are much easier to cut into than someone like Atlas. Proserpina mirrors my efforts on his left leg. Sometimes it can be nice to have a little help. Ceres, however, is on her own to trap Atlas. Being an older goddess, she has the best chance of going solo.

"Bacchus! Proserpina! Hold him there and stand clear!" My dad shouts as he soars into the air. The clouds above the battlefield darken and roar with thunder.

I feel a slight tingle through my hair as it begins to lift. "We gotta move!"

"No, Bacchus, we must hold Hyperion in place. If we back up, we might lose our grip on him." Proserpina holds her ground, unwavering. What an idiot.

I can't let her do this. Man, I hate being the hero. Rushing at full speed, I lunge at Proserpina, tackling her to the ground away from Hyperion. "I may be the god of madness, but you must be crazier than me!"

The vines on Hyperion's legs begin to loosen. "I'm getting free, Jupiter, make your shot count!" The mocking tone in his voice sends shockwaves of nerves through my body. Why is he so smug in the face of my dad's attack?

Before I can ponder any more, lightning strikes. The sky floods with neon blue light. A lightning bolt the size of the Titan himself smacks the ground with a massive *CRACK*! Even standing away from the blast sight, I can feel the electricity course through the earth beneath us.

"Uh. Thanks, Bacchus…" Proserpina gazes at where the Titan stood. Her breath sounds shaky. I can feel her body trembling as I hold her. Dad's power is terrifying.

He descends to our side. "Are you two all right?" We silently nod, still in awe.

All that is left at the blast site, that I can see, is a giant crater filled with a cloud of thick smoke. Hyperion must be dead; there's no way anyone could survive a hit like that. Almost as if the universe wanted to prove me wrong, a deep, maniacal laugh comes from the smoke.

"No…there's no way he survived! I hit him with all the lightning I could summon!" I've never heard my dad so panicked.

"Foolish god. False king. The traitorous son. You're powers seem weakened. I wonder why that could be." Hyperion's laugh rings terror through my head.

In response, almost on reflex, dad begins to ascend once more. "*AGH!*" Suddenly, he begins to rapidly descend and crashes back into the ground. "What...what have you done to me? What's wrong with my power?!"

"It is not what I have *done*. It is what your dear old father is *currently* doing!" As if on queue, the top of Mount Olympus explodes. His long dirty blonde hair falls back as his mocking laugh resumes.

I cup my hands over my head as it rages with pain. Through teary eyes, I see other Olympians are rendered in a similar state of painful paralysis. What have they done? They destroyed Olympus! Our seats of power, our thrones, that was their plan the entire time!

Without our seats of power, we Olympians are made useless. I can't feel the vines that surround us. My brain feels like it's being split apart. As if I'm going insane, but I can't control this madness. The last visual I see is the Titan Saturn, standing atop Olympus. Then, my vision goes black.

Chapter 14: Ballads of Apollo

My legs respond quicker than my mind. A loud explosion blasts the top of Mount Olympus behind us. I tackle Diana, shielding her from falling rocks. Boulder after boulder slams into my back. I use all my healing ability to repair my spine time after time. When the final rock hits, I collapse, falling next to my sister.

"Apollo...you saved me." Diana rushes to my side and grabs my hand. I don't know why I did it. Maybe I felt bad about her followers. Perhaps I'm not as self-centered as even I thought. Maybe I just wanted to protect her. "Stay here and rest. I will watch over you."

I stare up at her as my vision begins to blur. With her bow in hand, she stays alert for enemies from above. I never truly noticed how powerful she could be. One of my many misjudgments, I suppose. That changes today. She proved on the battlefield that she was the better archer, the better warrior. You'll never catch me saying any of this out loud, of course, but I think she landed more headshots than I did.

Concentrating my healing powers on my wounds, I feel nothing. No surge of energy in my veins. No relief from the tension in my muscles. I only feel intense pain. Every move I make sends a piercing shockwave through my spine.

"Diana!" Blood bursts from my mouth as I try to speak. "My healing, it's not working!"

The sky darkens as another boulder flies towards us. Diana nocks an arrow and fires at the boulder. And just like that she....misses? What?! Her face turns pale white as the boulder approaches. In one fell swoop, Diana snatches me off the ground and jumps from the cliffside, landing us on the ridge below.

"Nice shootin', Tex." In the face of adversity, at least I never lose my sense of humor. Laughing makes me cough up more blood as pain shoots through me once more.

Diana took a hardh breath, she was in no joking mood. "Not...the time. Shooting that arrow...I felt like I had never handled a bow in my life."

A painful scream fills the air. Is that Bacchus? My neck throbs as I force my head to turn. "Oh no..." Bacchus kneels hunched over, struggling to remain silent and still. Our dad lay weak and frail beside him. Proserpina loses all power over the plants around them as Hyperion walks free.

Each step from the Titan trembles the ground. His triumphant laughter rings through my mind. I spot Mercury standing still, struggling to catch his breath. Mars lays unconscious in another crater, his spear broken in two. Atlas runs his hands through his white hair as he looks over his work. I spot no signs of Minerva, they must have trapped her on the mountain.

Water sprays my face from the skies. Is it raining? Have even the elements turned against us? No, that's not it. A dark figure falls from the sky, hidden in the water. With my vision blurring by the second, it's hard to make out who it is.

He lands beside me, "Hey...nephew. We blew it this time, huh?" Neptune chokes on blood as he tries to speak. In the face of defeat, he never loses his wicked grin. But his eyes...they used to be as fierce as the raging ocean. Now they are calmed. I see no ocean.

"Venus's powers of persuasion don't seem to be working. Ceres and Juno are down for the count too." Diana, barely standing, assesses the battlefield once more. "Brother... uncle....we failed." And just like that, I black out.

Chapter 15: Saturn Rises

My blistered fingers grip hard stone as I scale the back of the mountain. I shrunk my body down to the size of those puny Olympians so my presence goes unnoticed. After we reclaim our place, I must thank Oceanus for slipping me through the seas while Neptune was distracted. Never knew he could be so strategic.

I reach the summit. Just as I expected, only Minerva and a few guards stand in my way now. These insolent gods think us fools. They believe we are without strategy, without plans, and that we only work on raw emotion. Maybe that was once true, but Tartarus has changed us. Made us stronger as we sat caged in that damned place.

"Hello, granddaughter." I approach the war room, swiping the insignificant guards aside.

Minerva's head whips around at the sound of my voice. It seems I have caught the goddess of battle strategy by surprise. "Saturn, I presume. How did you get up here? Does that mean-"

"Oh, the other Olympians are alive and fighting....for now. You thought we would all attack you head-on, didn't you?" Her shock amuses me. I suppose there's no harm in letting her know now. I've already won. "We got smarter, little one. We used your own bias against you. While we play into your pathetic trap, I slipped behind the mountain and climbed my way here."

"But why would you come-" Now she gets it. "The throne room! You're going to destroy the seats of power!" She reaches for her blade.

With a swipe of my hand, her movements come to a halt. Being the lord of time has its perks.

In my other hand, my golden scythe appears from thin air. Should I strike her down here and now? No, my revenge will be much more agonizing. A revenge in which all of the Olympians will suffer!

"Stay there, Minerva. This war will be over soon." A laugh from the deepest parts of my soul escapes me as I walk passed the young goddess, heading towards the throne room.

With a swipe of my scythe, I blast the doors off their hinges and send them flying across the room. So this is the mighty throne room of Olympus, eh? Pathetic. Just like all who stand against the mighty Saturn, Olympus will fall.

I grow my body, not to its original size, but big enough to smash through the ceiling. Now, with two final strikes, my vengeance will be realized. I swipe my scythe, destroying all the thrones to my left. Immediately, I follow with another strike to my right. The seats of power crumble beneath me as I continue my rampage on Olympus.

Boulders fall off the mountainside. I hope they crush some godlings on their descent. Roaring a triumphant laughter, I bask in the glory of my victory. Green flames encompass the top of the mountain, fields are destroyed, and homes explode. I am victorious!

I look over the battlefield. With this altitude, the entire field is in my vision. It's working. Olympians fall to their knees one after the other. Hyperion and Atlas raise their arms to salute me, the rightful ruler of the cosmos.

Scooping Minerva into my hand, I prepare for my descent. With no need to hide and no need for stealth, I jump from the mountain top. Growing to full size in the air, two craters form below my feet where I land.

"Excellent work, my king." Atlas, knowing his place, bows before me.

My eyes move to Hyperion as he mirrors Atlas. "Thank you for allowing us to partake in your ascension, my king."

"Yes, it is quite an honor for you two. You may stand tall, and be proud of our accomplishments today. Where is Oceanus?" My eyes trace the fields.

A wave of water crashes to my right. "Right here, brother." Oceanus emerges from the wave and kneels before me. His green eyes lower to the ground. The blue tint in his skin seems to have gotten paler over my years away. His long white beard moves with the winds.

"Good." I toss Minerva to the ground. "You two," I turn back to Atlas and Hyperion, "take these rejects to Tartarus. Chain them up as they did to us. Let's see how they like spending millennia in the deepest and darkest parts of Hades."

At the sound of my command, the two Titans collect the Olympians' unconscious bodies. All the years of torment, all the years of thirsting for revenge—it's all over now. Atlas and Hyperion leave to do my bidding.

Oceanus, staying behind, rises from his kneeling position. "It's time we returned home, brother. It's time we reclaim our thrones."

"You're right, Oceanus. It's time to return to Mount Othrys."

Chapter 16: Reign of the Titans

Entering the throne room of Mount Othrys, I feel at home at last. Sure, the place could use a bit of cleaning, but that's what mortals are for. After we call back all of our scattered brethren, we will begin our assault on the world. These mortals will finally know their proper place beneath their creators.

So far, only Titans that were locked in Tartarus, and a few stragglers, have returned. As of right now, it is just Oceanus, Atlas, Hyperion, Justitia, Jepetus, and I. Justitia and Jepetus were charged with securing our home while the rest of us crushed the Olympians. Soon, the whole family will be here. We will find those in hiding, those who betrayed us, and they will all submit to my will!

"Oceanus, the seas cover the majority of this planet. Use your wide range to start finding our lost brothers and sisters. It's time for them to return home." With a wave of my hand, my brother goes to carry out his orders.

With my scythe in hand and a new sense of pride and purpose, I finally sit upon my throne. A burst of power courses my veins as my position is reasserted. The last time I felt this happy was when I ascended the first time. Cutting my father, Uranus, to pieces and claiming his title of king. He once told me, in a dream-like vision, that the same would happen to me. But we are not the same. He's still scattered through the air, while I retake my place.

Atlas enters the throne room, kneeling before me. "Lord Saturn, we have chained the Olympians in Tartarus like you asked."

I sense hesitation in his voice. "But?"

"But, we seem to be missing some." He blurts out the confession.

"*Missing some?* How can we be missing an Olympian?! Did we not capture Pluto and then lay waste to Mount Olympus, fighting the other 11 in the process?!" My anger rises as fast as my thirst for answers.

Atlas cowers before me as I straighten in my throne. "Well... Pluto was never really an Olympian. Vesta gave up her throne for him apparently, but it was never made official. This is all according to him anyway. Your son is quite the talker. My guess is she was never anywhere near the battle and must have gone into hiding." My headache grows as I listen to this moron and his excuses. "And then there's Vulcan. Apparently, he was in his forge when we fought the battle. I sent Hyperion there to fetch him, but he came back empty-handed. There were no signs of anyone, according to Hyperion's report."

In a rage, I slash my scythe and destroy the nearest pillar. "Enough!" Of course, rising to power can never be easy. "Give me one good reason why I shouldn't kill you right now for your mistakes! Do you have *any* good news to bring?"

"Actually, sir, I do." He pulls out a scroll from his back pocket and begins to unravel it. "Hyperion found this in Vulcan's workshop. We think it's what he was trying to build for the battle." The scroll contains blueprints for a crown, one of immense power. "Luckily, we found his prototype as well and destroyed it."

"You *destroyed* it? Did you not for once think we could have used such power?" I hate to think of worst-case scenarios, but the Olympians, while chained in Tartarus, do still live. Even though the possibility of escaping is unlikely, we Titans did it.

Through frantic groveling, Atlas tries to excuse his mistakes once more. "I'm...I'm sorry,

Lord Saturn. I assumed we wouldn't require such a weapon. I'm an idiot, please spare me!" His cowardness sickens me.

"We never *require* more power, Atlas. But that doesn't stop me from wanting everything I can get. I do suppose your efforts on the battlefield proved partially useful. And you did still bring me the blueprints. Very well, you may remain free. But be warned, Atlas, all these excuses make you sound like your brother, Epimetheus. One more slip-up and I'll free him from your prison, and make you hold the world once more!" And just like that, he backs away, cleansing my sight of his presence.

Chapter 17: New World Order

Flames engulf the streets, the terrain is full of craters and destroyed earth, roads ripped up and undrivable. It's only been a few days since the Olympians fell but the world has fallen back into chaos. I stare up at the blood-red skies, wondering how we could have let this happen.

The man next to me stirs. He's finally waking. "Well, good morning, sleepy. Or is it night? I honestly can't tell anymore."

"Wha-where am I?!" He springs up from his cot, almost trampling over my fire.

I hand him a glass of water. "Sit, dear nephew. You're safe here. Rest by my hearth."

Vulcan's face of confusion turns to shock as I step into the light of the fire. "It's you! Even in those dirty monk robes, I'd recognize that red hair anywhere! What in the world are you doing here, Vesta? As a matter of fact, how did *I* get here?"

"Well, that's quite a long story. Gaze into the fire as I show you what has transpired." The fire grows as images begin to appear.

The battle at the base of Mount Olympus plays in its entirety. Flickering between each Olympian, one by one they lose the fight. Saturn commands his Titans to capture our family. Lastly, Hyperion ransacks Vulcan's forge.

"They destroyed everything. Our thrones... that's why I felt so much pain before passing out." With a start, he frantically searches his pockets. "Oh no! Whereisitwhereisitwhereisit!"

"Don't worry, Vulcan, it's safe." Reaching into my pockets, I pull out a small wooden box. "Your cyclops friend, he brought you to me when you collapsed. He dropped you off here this morning...or was it last night? Anyway, he gave me this wooden box. Told me nothing of its contents, only that it was important and only the rightful owner can open it." I toss it to him.

A sigh of relief escapes his soul. "That cyclops, I have to hand it to him, he outdid himself this time. In this box holds the key to our victory."

"Victory? Look around you, nephew. We have already lost. All we can do now is survive."

To my shock, he starts laughing. "We may have lost the battle, Vesta, but not the war. Even without our thrones, with this," He raises the box, "we have all the power we need to win. Speaking of which, how did you keep your powers? Olympus was destroyed."

It's my turn to laugh now. "I'm no longer an Olympian, remember? My seat of power no longer sits atop the mountain. Besides, glorified chairs aren't what gives a god their power."

"What do you mean? That's why we fell wasn't it?"

"It was, but not in the way you're thinking. The Olympians fell because of their own insecurities. We all put too much stock in our thrones of power, and at some point, we started seeing them as the *source* of our strength. Such foolishness. Were we not gods before Olympus was built? Did we not battle the Titans *before* claiming our places in the cosmos?" I raise my hands to my chin, staring into the fire.

Vulcan, scratching his head, "I don't know if I'm following you."

"Thrones don't make us gods, Vulcan. Worship doesn't make us gods. *Fate* makes us gods." I stare at my nephew through the flames.

"Then why did we lose our power when the thrones were destroyed?" It's like explaining things to a toddler sometimes.

"Did we? Did we really lose our power? Or did you just *believe* we did do to foolish ideas that crept their way into our minds over the centuries? Before you give me your answer, gaze into the hearth. Gaze into your soul."

Hesitantly, he leans into the hearth. I truly do not know what exactly he sees in the flames. We all have our demons, our own internal battles to fight. It is not my place to know them, only to bring warmth to the soul. A few minutes later, he emerges.

"I understand now." His fist ignites into a giant ball of fire. "My powers, they were inside me this whole time."

"Exactly, nephew, exactly." Finally, now there is hope.

He extinguishes his fist. "But doesn't this all just prove my point? We haven't lost yet. Yeah, our family is locked in Tartarus, but we aren't. We can free them, and get the box to them. We can still win!"

"Perhaps," I've never seen him so riled up, "But you know that I'm no fighter. I'm no warrior like my brothers and sisters. Not anymore, that is. Not after the *beast*. But *you* are, nephew. You do not need my help."

"But...I can't do this alone." His eagerness became dispair.

Poor boy still doesn't see the full picture. I guess I'll tell him. "You won't be alone. Where do you think the cyclops went? He's gathering allies. Minor gods and goddesses, anyone willing to help you sneak into Tartarus."

"Really?" Light returns to his eyes. "This is great news! I gotta give him a raise, I never knew he had this much fight in him. Most of the cyclopes folded into the service of the Titans before the war even started. Only a few stayed with me at the forge."

Now all that's left is to wait and rest. Hopefully, the cyclops will be back soon. Then maybe I can go back to my peace and quiet. I hate all this war, all the fights, and petty squabbling. Maybe the next go around we can be different. Next time, there could be a new world order.

Chapter 18: Depths of Tartarus

I awaken. Tugging at my muscles to move, the hot steel tightens against my body. My lips crack from lack of moisture, my body feels weakened and brittle. Around me, my family fair no better. Each tied to individual rock formations, we sit in a circle. The air is stiff and blisteringly hot, a faint orange hue fills my vision. This must be Tartarus.

"How are you fairing, brother." To my left, Jupiter's voice sounds raspy and dry. "The great sea god must not be doing so well in a damned place like this, huh."

When I look upon him, I do not see my brother, god of gods. All I see is a frail old man, bruised and beaten. "You look how I feel." A dry cough escapes me. "What happened?"

"We lost. Saturn destroyed Mount Olympus. At that moment, it was all over." He hangs his head in shame, locked in a staring match with the ground. "After that, Hyperion took us all here. He chained us in Tartarus to live out our eternal lives in torment."

My eyes make another swoop at the situation. Apollo, the poor sun god, looks worse than I. Being so far underground must be extremely draining for him. The rest look relatively okay, all things considered. A few bruises and scrapes here and there, but all seem as if their life force has been sucked out of them. These are the mighty Olympians, huh? Jupiter, myself, Juno, Ceres, Proserpina, Diana, Apollo, Mars, Pluto, Minerva, and Mercury. Wait...someone is missing.

"Where's Vulcan?" There are no signs of his presence anywhere in our new prison.

Pluto speaks up. "We don't know. He wasn't with the rest of you when Hyperion came." It dawns on me that Pluto must have been here the entire battle. He's been down here the longest of us all. "From what the others have told me, he was away from the battle, yes? Maybe he escaped his forges in time. Maybe he can finish his weapon."

That's putting a lot of faith in one Olympian. One that's not even our best fighter. Man, I wish it was Mars or even Minerva out there. That would be a way more reassuring thought. With our thrones destroyed, he most likely won't be able to craft anything. I pray to the Fates that he's able to finish his big secret weapon.

"So," I break the tension filling our prison, "anyone think of a plan to get out of here yet?"

"No, Neptune. There is no plan. There is no hope." Minerva's words send shivers down my spine. No plan? If even she has lost hope, what chance do we have?

"That's right!" A person slams into the center of our prison. Several of us cough as dirt and dust fill our lungs from the sudden force of wind. "There is no hope for you traitorous scum." As the dust cloud clears, Justitia emerges.

To my absolute surprise, Juno is the first to speak. "*You!* You dare call *us* traitors?! You turned your back on Olympus! You freed the Titans and brought chaos to the world!"

"I did what I had to in order to protect myself! You were going to betray me, Juno. Take away my domain!" Justitia's hair was a mess, her armor barely strapped on, deep bags beneath her eyes, and she was moving erratically. She's completely lost it.

Jupiter steps in to defend his wife. "Why in all the heavens would we do that?"

"For that!" She points her spear at Juno's stomach. "I heard what you told Ceres in her garden. I know what the fates foretold. That your child will bring about a *just* world. We all know what that means. He will adopt my domain as his own, pushing me to the side like...like I'm Sol or Luna." Her eyes shot daggers at Apollo and Diana.

Juno brings the attention back to her. "But we were friends, Justitia. I would *never* push you out of Olympus. We value you too much."

"HA! Don't waste your breath, Juno. You will not talk your way out of this one. I only came down here because I wanted to see it with my own eyes. I wanted to see the great Olympians chained and helpless." And with that great goodbye message, she flies off, back to the surface world.

What feels like an eternity passes. Every damned soul in Tartarus and their mothers came to mock us fallen Olympians. Some just watch, waiting for one of us to react. While others are more active with the humiliation. They take turns beating us, cutting us, even burning us. They especially like that last one with me. Then they feed us nectar, let us heal, and repeat.

As if the nonstop torture isn't enough, the air gets more unbearable by the minute. My body has no more moisture to sweat out, the only reprieve I get is from the nectar, but that just makes things worse. The short burst of hope that hydration gives is quickly taken away. Time after time my spirit is broken. Death would be far kinder than this.

Chapter 19: Anguish of the Gods

My vision blurs and swirls. Exerting all of my willpower to remain conscious is such a tiring chore. This place...these sunless lands...it drains me as much it does my uncle. There's light here, yes, but it is of a different source. Sunlight is pure and breathes life. Tartarus, while just as natural, sucks the life from your pores. It's evil, twisted, and blistering.

As if that wasn't enough for my plight, we seem to have become quite the entertainment down here. Monsters of all shapes, sizes, and smells come from far and wide to see the mighty Olympians chained and broken. I don't even know how long we've been down here, but it feels like an eternity.

A mighty roar shakes me back to the present. My body trembles as a manticore jumps into the circle. The beast thrashes around his scorpion tail. It grazes Mercury's arm and sinks into my chest. A fiery sensation pulses through my veins as the manticore's poison enters my system. Our screams are silenced by the roaring applause from the onlookers. I aim to please my fans.

Instead of giving me the mercy of blacking out, nectar is forced down my throat once more. The hole in my chest pieces itself back together rapidly. My vision returns as renewed life enters my body. Tears trace my cheeks. This is the worst part of our torment.

The manticore continues its rampage. This time around, however, it seems to be using its claws instead of its tail. How thoughtful. Mars hollers a blood-curdling scream as the manticore rips into his torso. Slash marks tore through his skin and muscle. The monster exits the circle, leaving Mars to suffer. My eyes pull away from the gruesome scene.

Bacchus shakes in his chains, muttering incoherently to himself in ancient greek. He's been like this ever since we got here. Barely any of the monsters torture him; they get plenty of pleasure watching him do it to himself. The god of madness, brought down by his own domain.

My dad and Juno receive the worst punishment. As the king and queen of the Olympians, they are always the first targets when new torturers appear. Dad has wronged them all in some way, shape, or form over the millennia, and now is their chance for vengeance. They try and try to fight back, but, like the rest of us, their will is shattered. I'm sure we are all thinking the same thing: "What's the point?"

Next to me, my sister Diana is the only one who remains strong in spirit. If a monster gets too close, she'll bite, spit, headbutt, and do whatever she can to fight back. Her determination in the face of defeat is awe-inspiring. I only wish it was worth her efforts.

Finally, they give us a reprieve. They feed drops of nectar to Mars and whoever else is fatally wounded, but only just enough to keep us conscious. Any wounds left are for us to deal with as we await another round of "playtime." After the last drops are administered, our captors leave.

"Well, that was fun." I break the harsh silence.

Mars lets out a deep but hollow laugh. "Oh yeah, it was a blast." His laughs turn to coughs as he chokes on each word. "I think this might be my new vacation spot."

"Humor at a time like this, Mars? Careful now, brother, you might be walking into my territory." Really, though, this isn't like him to play along.

My concerned thoughts are interrupted by the sound of Venus chuckling. To my absolute amazement, she seems relatively unharmed. Did the monsters just forget about her? No, they hate us all; they wouldn't want to leave anyone out of their revenge. It can't be from the nectar; they don't give us enough to heal all of our wounds. Come to think of it, I didn't hear her once since being down here. I wonder why that is.

Chapter 20: A Titan's Choice

Water drips from my brow as the heat of Tartarus intensifies. I thought I had no more sweat to give, but the nectar they forced into us must have restored my hydration a bit. For some reason, the monsters have taken it easy on me. I do not know their motives, but it can't be good.

Mars struggles to breathe next to me. My poor lover, I wouldn't wish this torture on anyone. Not even my oaf husband, Vulcan. Oh my....Vulcan...that's right, he's still out there. I wonder if he's been captured already. No, they would have brought him here immediately. Does this mean there is still hope? Vulcan may be an overcompensating ass, but I've never once doubted his work and will of fire.

"So," Apollo strains his vocal cords, "Why are you so special, Venus?"

My head hangs in shame. "I do not know, Apollo. I am just as clueless as you are, I'm afraid." Of course I do not wish to be tortured, but being the only one left untouched while my family suffers? To me, that's the worst kind of punishment.

"Well, allow me to enlighten you then." Oh, great. Justitia appears, returning to our prison.

I, being the elegant goddess that I am, spit at her. "You've got some nerve, showing your face around here again."

"Now now, Venus. Is that any way to thank me? Any way to repay the debt you owe?" She steps closer with each word.

"Debt? What debt? The only thing I owe you is a blade to the neck when we get out of here!" I don't know where this fight in me is coming from, but a burning hatred sears its way into my soul.

Apollo shouts from his post, "What is she talking about, Venus?" Jutsitia waves her hand. A red cloth appears and covers his mouth. As quickly as he speaks, he is silenced.

"Silence! The grownups are talking." Grinning, she kneels in front of me. "I'm the one who told the monsters to leave you be. I kept you safe. Well, as safe as you can be in Tartarus anyway."

Our eyes meet. "Why me? Why do you single me out? What could you possibly gain from protecting me?"

"Because you're like me, Venus. A Titan playing hero by siding with the Olympians." She looks around at the others with disdain.

"I *AM* an Olympian! I'm nothing like you; I wouldn't betray those I care about!" My face burns red hot; hatred rises within me with every word she utters.

"By name and status, yes, you are an Olympian. But do not forget your parentage. You were born from Uranus. You are closer to us Titans in the generational chain than you are to these puny deities." She makes a point, I never put too much stock in parentage, but when you think of it like that...

I steele my resolve. "While your words may ring true, Justitia, it still does not explain your motives."

"Isn't it obvious? This is a new age. An age of Titans. *All* Titans." Her eyes dig into my soul. "Join us. You can be free of your chains. Free of these would be gods. Assume your rightful place with the Titans."

She now stands face to face, almost touching me. Her mistake. "I told you once, and I'll say it again. I. AM. AN. OLYMPIAN!" With all the force I can muster, I smash my forehead into hers—silver blood leaks from both of our heads.

"So be it then. You get no more favors from me. You've made your choice." She disappears as quickly as she came.

Mars, barely conscious, speaks out. "You know I've always loved that fiery side of yours." He coughs up more blood. "But that was probably stupid. Now, you'll be tortured like the rest of us."

"Then so be it." My tone shocks me. Where did this come from? My years spent with Mars must have rubbed off on me. "I'd rather die with my chosen family than live lying to myself."

"You're right." Jupiter, who I long thought passed out with the others, speaks softly and assuredly. "You truly are an Olympian, Venus. None of us would ever question your loyalty."

His words, while kind, do not sound like the Jupiter I know. He's never been this soft-spoken, at least not to me. His voice used to be brimming with confidence and authority. I hear none of that now. Tartarus has taken its toll on us all, but I fear what it has done to our king.

Chapter 21: Escape From Tartarus

The harsh wind knocks dust into my eyes. Unable to see who has landed, I can only assume it's *her*. "Come back to gloat again, Justitia? Haven't you had enough?"

"Oh, on the contrary, uncle. We are just getting started." That voice, it's deep and raspy. This isn't Justitia.

As my eyesight clears, the mystery man comes into focus. "*Vulcan?!*" I can't believe my eyes. Standing in front of me is my nephew. And...is that? Floating above Vulcan is a pale, skinny man with a long black robe and blinding white wings. "Letum...."

"Hello again, Lord Pluto. Vulcan and I are here to rescue you. We must return order to the world." He elegantly floats down by my side and unlocks my chains.

"I'll explain everything on the way out. First, we must wake up and free the rest of the Olympians. Take this." Vulcan tosses me a vile of nectar.

Drinking the nectar is bittersweet. After being tortured with its healing properties for so long, I can hardly believe we are escaping at last. That vile was enough to restore my health and strength. Following Vulcan's orders, I begin waking my brethren.

The Olympians are freed one by one. After drinking the nectar, almost all of us are back in good shape. Unfortunately, the small vials aren't enough to fully heal Mars and Apollo's wounds. Not to mention Bacchus; nectar does little for mental wounds, I'm afraid.

Bacchus stands in place, looking at the ground. His body trembles as he mutters, "No...not the frogs....I hear the frogs....their coming back..."

"My son!" Jupiter's shout breaks my eyes from the pitiful sight. He squeezes Vulcan in a tight embrace. "You have done well." This place really has changed him. Quite frankly, it's weirding me out.

"All right, all right. Save the hugs for later." This touchy stuff was taking too long; I had to end it. "We have to get moving. Vulcan, what's your plan to get us out?"

Vulcan clears his throat. "First thing's first." He tosses a glass ball filled with flames onto the ground. As the ball shatters, a roaring fire blazes, but it does not harm us. It feels...like home.

Apollo steps forward, placing his hands on his hips. "Fire? That's your plan?"

Vulcan pushes him aside. "Not just any fire. This is fire from Vesta's hearth. She looked after me and reminded me of who I am. Who we *all* are. Now it's time for you to remember, too." He gestures at the fire expectantly.

I gaze into the flames. That's....me? In the fire, images of my entire life flashes before my eyes. Scenes of my time in the underworld with Proserpina, our wedding, and horrors from the time my siblings and I were trapped in Saturn's stomach. Lastly, images of our first war against the Titans, we hadn't even built Olympus or my palace yet. We had only just escaped our father. Wait... that's right, this was *before* our seats of power.

"I understand now." My eyes move from the fire. My power feels rejuvenated. It feels stronger than it ever has. I summon my bident and my helm of darkness. "I'm ready."

"As am I." Jupiter, back with his old cocky grin, ignites lightning in his palms. "What say you, Olympians!"

One after another, we each roar with approval. If the others feel as empowered as I do, we might be able to take back our world. Together, we all might have a shot. Not everyone seems as assured as I do, though.

Juno sulks next to her husband. "What makes you think this time will be any different? We *barely* won the first war and got annihilated the second they rose again. Nothing has changed."

"You're wrong." Vulcan, reaching into his pocket, steps towards her. "This time, we have this! Behold!" He raises in his palm a....wooden box?

"What's in the booooox?!" Apollo squeals next to me. Groaning in disapproval, I smack the back of his head.

Vulcan hands the box to Juno. "This is what I've been working on. The secret to our victory. Open it, Mom."

Golden light shines through the crack as Juno opens her gift. She pulls out the most elegant gold crown I have ever seen. As she places it atop her head, the golden light continues to pulse around her body. No, around us all. I look at my hands; my skin is outlined with a faint golden glow. I feel incredible, powerful even.

Vulcan, putting on his salesman voice, "This is no ordinary crown, as you all may now be realizing. When worn by its proper owner, the crown will radiate a healing and protecting light. Our wounds, if we can even accumulate any, will be healed in an instant. The ultimate defense."

Chapter 22: Rebirth

Normally, I'd say escaping Tartarus is an impossible task. With the crown, however, it's proving to be a nice warm-up for our real fight. I knew I was a good blacksmith, but I may have really outdone myself on this one. Hordes of monsters block our exit; all perish before our might.

Up ahead, about 20 empussa block the next tunnel. Dad waves us aside, summoning a bright and powerful bolt of lightning. *CRACK!* The empussa stood no chance against my dad's strength. They flop on the ground like fish out of water, electricity coursing through their bodies.

Before we can exit this damned domain, a manticore blocks our path. Without hesitation, Mars and Apollo spring into action. Apollo, with his incredible accuracy, shoots an arrow through each of the beast's eyes. Mars charges the creature as it thrashes wildly. Using the monster's giant paw as leverage, he jumps onto the manticore's back and grabs its scorpion tail. Mars drives the manticore's stinger straight into the beast's own back.

The manticore slumps over, dead. I've never seen them so in sync before. Mars walks back to the group, nodding to Apollo. No words need be spoken; that was personal for them. We continue.

Leaving Tartarus and entering the realm of Hades, a wave of relief washed over me. The hardest part, the final battle, is still coming, but at least we can breathe easy from here on. Now that my uncle is back at full power, no one in his realm will dare challenge us.

Finally, we arrive at Pluto's palace. The place was a wreck. Walls were destroyed to rubble, and a giant crack in the ground split the throne room in two. This must be where Pluto took his stand against the Titians, sending Mercury off to warn us. Sometimes, I forget just how powerful he can be.

"Well, then," Pluto speaks up, "Welcome to my home. Sorry for the mess; my last guests were a bit unruly." He sits on what is left of his throne.

Minerva takes control of the room. "We need a plan. Even with our newfound strength and defensive power, we still can't just rush in blind." All the Olympians nod in agreement. "We underestimated our opponent last time; we will *not* do so again."

"What do you suggest then, daughter." Dad runs his fingers through his beard.

"I say we take a page from the Titans' book. They are bound to know by now, if not soon, that we have escaped. Saturn knows that we are attached to Mount Olympus and our seats of power. Or at least, we *were*." She looks at me, "Thank you for reminding us that we are not as attached as we once thought."

My gaze turns to the floor. "No problem," I grumble. I'm not used to the Olympians complimenting me.

"Saturn probably thinks our first plan of action will be to take back Mount Olympus. He probably already has his Titans guarding the place." She rubs her chin, "I say we feed into his delusions while simultaneously taking a page out of his book."

Apollo raises his hand, "I'm not entirely sure that I follow you."

"Idiot," Mars folds his arms, "She's saying we will attack Olympus like Saturn expects us to. All while a small group of us heads to Mount Othrys to attack Saturn, who presumably would stay safe in his throne room."

Minerva looks approvingly at her war counterpart. "Pretty close, Mars. The thing is, though, we need to make him believe *all* of us are attacking Olympus. We will put up a fight, displaying all of our power to the heavens. Then, in the midst of battle, a small team will slip away and head to Mount Othrys."

"I will be part of this team," My dad's voice is full of authority, telling us this is not up for debate. "Pluto and Neptune will come with me."

At the sound of their names, Pluto and Neptune move to his side. It makes sense for it to be them. The three most powerful gods, taking on the most powerful Titan. I like our odds a lot. Even without the crown's protection, they can beat him as they did many millennia ago.

"Now that the plan is settled. There is something else we must discuss." Mom steps into the spotlight. "What happens *after* we defeat the Titans."

Dad raises an eyebrow, "What do you mean, my wife? What is there to discuss?" He places his arm around her.

"When we take back the world from the Titans, we will have to rebuild. Not just Mount Olympus, but the mortal world too. We must renew their faith in us. We can't be as we once were. Arrogant, ill-tempered, petty. What makes us any different than the Titans when we act this way?" She looks out to all of us, gazing into our souls.

Dad squeezes her tightly. "I agree with you." A collective gasp fills the room. "What? After spending time in Tartarus, I thought over and over again about what led us here. What we...what *I* could have possibly done for us to deserve such torment. I have not been the best king. Hades, I haven't been the best father or husband." He looks at mom. "Things will be different. This is not just our resurrection. It will be our rebirth." With those final words, we prepare for battle.

Chapter 23: March on Olympus

Thinking about the coming battle, scorching rage flows through my veins. They dare make fools of us? Make a fool of *me*? These Titans are about to see first-hand why they call me the god of war! My vengeance will be glorious. Today, the Titans fall one final time.

Hoping to keep some element of surprise, we decided to head to Olympus on foot. Twelve gods flying through the air would be far too noticeable. The Titans know we are coming, but they don't know when. The portals were destroyed with Mount Olympus, so that was always out of the question.

Now of sound mind, Bacchus works with Ceres and Proserpina to keep our cover. Hiking through fields of tall grass and forests, we march on. Mercury runs slightly ahead of the group, using his incredible speed to scout for enemies. So far, so good.

We enter the forest below Mount Olympus. The shadows of towering Titans darken the terrain. If I were a betting man, I'd wager all the Titan warriors showed up. It's time for battle.

Stepping out of the woods, our prey eagerly awaits their demise. Quickly scanning the battlefield, they have no armies of monsters here. The only enemies to fight are the Titans themselves. Atlas, Hyperion, Japetus, and Crius stand tall, ready for combat. Looking at Crius, his eyes remind me of a starry night sky, his skin almost as pale white as Letum, but with a gray tint. His hair reminds me of Pluto. I'd hate to keep them waiting.

"Prepare yourselves!" I point my spear, aiming it specifically at Atlas.

At the wave of father's hand, Neptune jumps into the nearby ocean. He has his own revenge to get. Oceanus won't even know what hit him. Right now, however, my focus is on one Titan and one Titan only. Atlas.

Father turns to us. "Olympians! Let's take back our home! Take back our world! For Olympus!" Raising our weapons high, we roar in unison.

"Yell all you want," Atlas speaks at last, "We all know how this battle ends."

I sprint at my opponent. "Yeah, with you back in your prison!"

Father blows a gust of wind beneath me, boosting my jump into the air. Putting as much force as I can, I launch my spear from my hands.

With my altitude, I should be able to reach his neck. Atlas goes to swipe the weapon from the air, but the spear is knocked off course before he can. An arrow shot by Apollo scrapes the bottom of the metal, changing its direction upward. Narrowly passing through the Titan's large fingers, the spear sinks into his eye.

"*AGH!*" Atlas rips the spear out of his dark eye, spraying silver blood all over the battlefield.

I land on the ground, continuing my assault. "Bacchus, he's blinded! Quickly, trap him there!" My brother heads my command.

Once again, wrapping the Titan's legs in vines, Baccus holds him. Using the vines as leverage, I climb his leg. The moment I reach his torso, I pull the dagger from my back pocket and embed it into his stomach. Pushing the blade deep into his skin, I leave only the hilt visible.

"TAKE THIS!" I push my feet off the vines and fall towards the ground. My dagger, still inside Atlas, gashes his stomach open. Looking at him, I wince in pain where my old manticore wounds once were.

All around me, the battle rages on. Father and a shrunken Crius engage in an intense aerial fight. Lightning and shooting stars light up the skies. Each moving too fast for my eyes to see. *CRACK!* Every collision is met with tiny explosions.

Proserpina and Pluto take on the green Titan, Japetus. Diana, from afar, launches arrow after arrow, giving ample cover fire. They use a similar strategy to Apollo, Bacchus, and I. Prosperina holds the goliath still while Pluto strikes with his bident. Skeletal warriors pry their way from the dirt to help their master. Diana, beside her twin, rains arrows on Japetus's bald head. Vulcan joins the fray and launches fireball after fireball at the Titan's torso, knocking Japetus back.

Hyperion, with all his strength, required the most teamwork. Ceres struggles to keep the Titan locked in her vines; Hyperion is too smart for that. Every time she ties him up, he immediately cuts the vines with his bronze blade. While she may not be able to bind the Titan, she at least is distracting him. Letum flies above Hyperion, striking from the skies with his sword. Mother, Venus, and Minerva strike in perfect harmony. First, Minerva slashes Hyperion's ankle with her sword. Following close behind, mother uses her dagger to take out the other ankle. Finally, being hoisted by Minerva's shield, my darling Venus launches herself at the Titan. She sinks her dagger into Hyperion's thigh and, like me, uses the inertia of her fall to slice him open. The golden Titan falls to one knee.

Giant tidal waves crash into each other as the fight between Neptune and Oceanus rages on. I can't see much of what's actually happening, only what it looks like on the surface. The ocean stirs, not knowing which master's commands to obey. It's a miracle the battlefield hasn't been flooded yet.

"Look out!" My mind snaps back to the task at hand as Mercury pushes me to the side.

In doing so, he takes the hit intended for me. A giant fist blocks out the sun and crashes down on top of my brother. Atlas roars with laughter as he squashes Mercury like a bug. In the crater, Mercury lays still. I rush to his side.

"Mercury! Are you okay?! You saved me!" Examining him, both his legs have been crushed and broken at the knees.

The same golden light from before radiates around him. He becomes warm to the touch. *SNAP!* Looking at his broken legs once more, they've magically snapped themselves back into place. Slowly but surely, the bruises and cuts on his face close and heal.

Mercury stands up, taking a wobbly step forward. "I'm just," he catches his breath, "I'm just glad the crown seems to be working. That hurt."

"Go to Apollo, make sure your legs are good, and gather your energy. You've done well in this battle, brother." I smack his back, sending him on his way to the others.

Atlas abruptly stops his laughter, he must have realized his mistake. "How are you still running, godling? Looks like I'll have to break you again!" He lifts his foot to stomp on Mercury.

"Oh no you don't, ugly!" Summoning a new spear to me, I focus my power through it.

The spear glows a bright red and gold as it begins to grow exponentially. I position myself in the shadows of the giant foot. As Atlas continues with his stomp, my spear penetrates through the bottom. Like stepping on the world's biggest thumbtack. I roll out of the way to not get myself squashed, but it's far too late for the Titan to stop. Gravity ensures that he sees his actions through.

"We aren't just some 'puny godlings,' Atlas! We are the Olympians!" My onslaught resumes.

Minerva's plan is working so far. Mother's crown is protecting us, allowing us not to hold back. The Titans still don't realize how futile their attacks truly are. Now if we can keep this ruse going, father, Neptune, and Pluto should have no issues sneaking away to fight Saturn. There's no way father can lose to Crius. No way Neptune will relinquish his domain to Oceanus. The Olympians will see victory today. I will ensure it!

Chapter 24: Titans Betrayal

Watching the battle through flames in my chambers, a sense of unease fills me. Due to recent events, Saturn has taken me off soldier duty, leaving me here to watch. These days, it takes all of my willpower just to remain sane. Often, I find myself questioning my own judgment. It doesn't help that my nagging counterpart keeps barging into my room.

"Hello, Justitia." The sickly woman limps into my room. Her frail body can barely support her and her skin looks as if it were melting off of her bones. Her head is full of white patchy hair where beautiful black hair used to grow.

Looking at her makes me sick. "What do you want now, Invidia? Here to give me another lecture?"

"I'm here because it's where I'm needed." She collapses onto the chair in the corner.

I scoff, "Needed? I do not require any assistance from *you*. You can barely even stand on your own two legs."

"You know fully well why I'm like this, Justitia." She coughs violently, wheezing to oxygenate her lungs.

"Oh yes, you're ridiculous theory..." Staring into the fire, something nags in my head. Is it just a theory? Or could there be truth to it?

Invidia, using what I can only assume is all of her strength, tosses her cane at my head. "Look at me! I'm like this because of *you*! The moment you decided to help Saturn, you turned your back on justice! You crept your way into *my* domain!" She points to the fire. "Look what you have wrought!"

Screaming comes from the flames, bringing my attention back to the important matters. Juno keels over, clutching her stomach as she sobs with pain. Mercury rushes to her aid, kneeling by her side.

"What is it, Juno? What happened?!" He panics, unable to locate a wound.

Her voice cracks with agony as she commands the god of speed. "The baby! Something's wrong! Take me to Apollo, quickly!"

Invidia snaps me back to my room. "Does this look *just* to you? To me, it looks more like vengeance."

"No! You're wrong!" My hands clutch my temples as I wail in protest.

"You eavesdropped on a conversation, hearing only *part* of what was said. You tapped into the powers of prophecy and *assumed* what it meant. You used what could mean anything as an excuse to let loose the biggest villain in our entire history! Now, Juno is on the verge of losing her child. YOUR friend!" Gripping the sides of her chair, she stands up. 'Tell me, Titaness of Justice, what about any of this is just?"

With my nails clawing at my head, I fall to my knees. She can't be right. I do not act out of revenge. I only punish those who must be punished. I bring justice to the world. AHH!

No....maybe...maybe *I'm* wrong. Juno's screams ring through my head like a siren. She was my friend. They *all* were my friends. The fog in my head begins to clear. I can see the light. Wait....I really can see a light. What's happening to me?

A blinding white light engulfs my body. When my vision returns, I find myself not hunched over in my room but on the battlefield. Juno, Apollo, and Mercury do not notice my presence. They are too focused on Juno's pain.

"I'm sorry, my queen." Apollo removes his hand from her stomach. "The child will not survive. There's nothing even I, the god of healers, can do now. The strain on your body has just been too much."

I know what I must do. Taking a step forward, I make my presence known. "Juno...I....I'm so sorry." Sobbing, I collapse beside her.

"YOU! What are you doing here!" Crawling back, Juno distances herself. "This is all your fault," she sobs, "You did this to us! You did this to *me*!"

Reaching my hand out, I place it on hers. "I know. This *is* my fault. I misunderstood something

I had no business being involved with in the first place. But I think I understand now. I know how I can fix this. I understand what the prophecy means."

"Wha-" Before she can finish her sentence, my scales fall from my pocket, crashing onto the ground as my body goes limp. A bright white light leaves my body and enters Juno. The visions that started this all fill my head one final time. I can only smile. Goodbye, my friend.

Chapter 25: Gods and Titans

Using the winds to accelerate my arm, I punch Crius in his gray jaw. "Give it up, Titan. You can't beat me. Especially not in my realm." Crius spirals through the air wildly before catching himself.

"You may claim domain over the skies, Jupiter, but the stars are mine!" Crius raises his arms high above his head.

The skies turn from their deep-red stain into a starry night sky. The constellations begin to bend to his will. The Saggitarius draws back its bow, aiming its arrow at me. Shooting stars form the shape of the arrow as it's fired. Bracing myself, I prepare for impact.

A star grazes my face, cutting my cheek. Thanks to my wife's new crown, the wound immediately begins to heal. Wait....where is Juno, anyway? Weaving my way through Crius's barrage, I scan the battlefield below. My eyes widen. She's lying beside Apollo, unconscious. What happened to my wife?!

I must end this fight quickly. Turning my attention back to Crius, my rage shall fuel my attack. Stretching my arms out wide, I feel the winds through my hair and static surging through my fingertips. With a thunderous clap of my palms, a wall of lightning fires directly at the Titan. He tries to escape, but he's too slow. My attack collides, sending Crius spiraling to the ground, his body convulsing rapidly. He's not getting back up from that.

Red stains the skies once more. I race towards my wife. Something must have happened to her in the battle. Earlier I heard a faint scream….could it have been her? Up in the air, using my powers, it can be hard to hear those on the ground. I hope whatever it is, we can fix it.

"What happened?!" My feet indent themselves into the ground with my harsh landing. "Apollo, explain!"

He placed a hand on my shoulder. 'First of all, she's okay. Right now, she is just unconscious, but she will be fine." Relief washes over me at the sound of my son's words. "But there's still something you should know."

"What is it?" Kneeling beside my wife, I place my hand in hers.

"Well, it's honestly hard to explain. I'm still wrapping my head around this." He scratches his forehead. "Juno came to me hurt. She told me she felt something was wrong with the baby. She was right." My expression must have been telling. Apollo holds up his hands, "Whoa whoa! Let me finish! Yes, when I checked on her, it seemed like the baby was gone. The stress from Tartarus, the battles, it all took its toll on her body. But then, out of nowhere, Justitia just *appears* before us." He gestures to the Titaness's motionless body. The orange tint fades from her skin. "She told us that she was sorry, that she finally understood what the prophecy meant. Then...I honestly don't know what happened." His confusion returns. "Justitia grabbed Juno's arm, and all of a sudden, this bright white light left Justitia's body and entered Juno."

"*Entered* Juno?" Now I'm equally as lost.

Apollo shrugs, "Then Justitia just died, and Juno was knocked unconscious. And I mean like *died* died, like she was some mortal."

"And what of Juno? What of our child? You said it *seemed* like it was lost." My confusion grows.

He kneels beside me, "Juno is fine. I do not sense any harm was done to her. She will wake up soon. As for the baby," A grin widens on his face, "The baby is perfectly healthy! It's a real medical miracle!"

'What?!" My confusion is quickly replaced with joy. "So, they are both going to be okay?"

"Yes, dad, they will be okay. If I were to make an educated guess, Justitia must've focused the rest of her lifeforce, her spirit, on the child. Giving it the lifetime she would have lived. The ultimate sacrifice." Apollo rises to his feet. "I'm sorry, but you must leave now. The battle continues. I will watch over them." He draws his bow, guarding Juno.

Placing Juno's hand down gently, I rise. "You're correct, son. Thank you for taking care of her. I know you two haven't always gotten along."

"Hey, *rebirth*, right?" At his words, I nod in silent understanding.

Launching myself back into the air, I search for where I am needed most. Neptune still battles his nemesis in the ocean. Typhoons clash, and giant sea monsters wrestle in the waters as tidal waves hit the coast. I dare not interfere with my brother's fight. This is personal for him, and I must respect that.

Bacchus seems to have taken a more aggressive approach now that Mars's spear traps Atlas. Vines slither around the Titan's throat, squeezing tight. Mars, using his daggers, scales the Titan's back. I never knew those two could be such a fierce duo.

Atlas begins to thrash around, trying to shake Mars off his back. The god of war persists in his climb. Using his sunken daggers as leverage, he propels his body farther up the Titan's back. Resummoning his daggers just before he lands, he sinks them into Atlas's flesh. However, once he reaches the Titan's head, things take a turn. Atlas shakes Mars off, but not before both daggers sink into his skull. His white hair slightly darkens as the silver blood pours out.

"Bacchus, catch Mars! I have an idea!" Bacchus heads my command and springs into action. Grabbing Mars out of the air with a vine, he places his brother gently on the ground.

The plan is clear as day. With Mars's spear in the Titan's foot and his daggers in the Titan's head, Atlas just became the perfect conductor. Lightning once again fills my palms. Pulsing with power, I fire a beam of electricity from each hand. My left aims for the spear, my right the daggers.

Electricity surges through the metal, frying Atlas from the inside out. The Titan falls onto his back, rendered unconscious. It's over for Atlas. After all this is said and done, I will personally ensure he returns to his prison. The war isn't over yet.

In the distance, more enemies appear. I can't make them all out, but I recognize some of my old foes. A few of the remaining Titans, Dione and Tethys, walk toward the battle. Marching beside them, hordes of monsters approach.

"Father!" Minerva calls to me, leaving Hyperion to the others.

I descend from the skies and land beside her, "More enemies are coming. Two more Titans and another monster army."

"I know. That means our plan is working. Saturn has seen we are all here and fighting. Now is your chance to slip away. Get Pluto and Neptune, then go." Normally, I hate being commanded by my children. This time, however, she's right.

I grab Pluto and fly us to the shore. Neptune and Oceanus are still battling hard, but that fight with Atlas has given me an idea. First things first, Neptune needs to get out of the water, or else my plan might fry him, too. As much as I'd love to see that, we need him conscious. We land on the beach.

"Neptune!" Cupping my hands around my mouth, I amplify my voice. "Fall back!"

A column of water splashes beside us. Neptune steps out, "What is it, brother? I'm kind of busy here."

Without a word, I take to the skies once more. Dark clouds surround me, covering the landscape in darkness. Lightning rains down from each cloud in rapid-fire succession, electrifying the water so intensely that no living thing could survive. Oceanus floats to the top of the water, motionless.

"Excuse you!" Neptune calls from the shores. "I believe that was *my* fight!"

I land beside him, "Sorry, brother, but there's no time. Minerva's plan is working. Titan reinforcements will arrive any second. I saw Dione, Tethys, and their armies marching forth. Now it is time for us to defeat our father once more."

Without hesitation, we head to Mount Othrys. It's finally time to end this war once and for all.

Chapter 26: Final Battle

Neptune, on his chariot pulled by seahorses, rides beside me. Pluto opted to catch a ride with Neptune as he thinks me carrying him through the air is "too demeaning." Although, I don't think he's having much of a better time with Neptune. Pluto's always been such a sour sport.

Nevertheless, we all have one goal; one target. Our father will pay for what he has done to us and for what he has done to the world. Saturn falls today. All of the Titans will feel the wrath of Olympus!

Up ahead of us, Mount Othrys comes into view. Saturn has already sent his reinforcements to the battle on Olympus; he'll be alone here. My brothers and I defeated him once before; I have zero doubts about our ability to do so again. My brothers and I approach the mountain.

Grabbing Neptune and Pluto, I fly us to the summit. No one intercepts us as we enter the palace. Having no need to be stealthy, we rush to the throne room. There he is, sitting upon his throne.

"Hello, father." Pluto steps in front of us. "Are you ready to return to Tartarus?"

Saturn's eyes widen. "What?! How did you three get here?!"

"Surprised to see us? We just used your own plan against you. Your arrogance will lead to your downfall!" To make his point, Neptune slams his trident into the floor, cracking the marble.

His shocked expression morphs into a sadistic grin. "No matter. I will just crush you all here and now!"

Saturn, scythe in hand, lunges at us. I grab the collars of my older brothers' shirts and push them to the ground. We narrowly dodge our father's attack as he flies right over us. This is no time to get cocky.

Jumping to my feet, Neptune follows suit. In the corner of my eye, Pluto dawns his helm of darkness and slips into the shadows. It's up to Neptune and I to keep Saturn's attention. That shouldn't be too difficult.

"You're getting slow, old man," I say. "Pretty soon, you'll need to use that scythe as a cain."

Saturn's nostrils flare, and his eyes fill with rage. He throws his scythe. Using the flat of his blade as leverage, I launch myself at him. Again, using the winds to amplify my inertia, I punch him in the chest. Saturn flies back, crashing through the walls of the palace. Crumbled pieces of brick-red rock scatters on the floor where Saturn once stood.

Neptune summons a wave of water underneath us. He uses his undeniable command of the seas to glide us into the room where Saturn lay flat. Knocked down on his back, this is our time to strike. My brother jumps from the water, aiming his trident directly at our father's torso.

Saturn rolls out of the way, leaving Neptune's trident to sink into the marble. Of course, it can never just be that easy for us. Saturn lands a powerful kick on Neptune, sending him spiraling into me. We both crash against the wall.

Behind Saturn, however, Pluto reemerges from the shadows. He takes his opportunity to sneak attack the Titan king. Pulling his bident out of the darkness, he impales Saturn in the back. The Titan screams in pain as Pluto pushes the bident through him. My brother doesn't stop until the two-pronged spear is out the other side.

"Good work, Pluto!" Catching my breath from the impact, I stand. The magic from Juno's crown must not reach us here. "Neptune, you could take a few notes."

Neptune wipes the dust off his shirt. "Ha Ha. I see where Apollo gets that annoying humor from." He summons his trident to him. "Now, can we get back to the matter at hand?"

"Puny gods." Saturn rises to his feet. "Failed spawn. You think you can defeat me that easily?"

At that moment, the scythe came spiraling back to him. This will be the final time he gets to wield his weapon. Glancing between my brothers, we all ready ourselves for this fight. Pluto reaches into the darkness and retrieves a pitch black shortsword. Haven't seen him use that thing in centuries, I hope he still knows how to wield it. Neptune readies his trident.

Summoning lighting to my hands, I launch the first attack. Saturn tries to slash at me, but his scythe is quickly stopped by Neptune. My brother locks the scythe between the trident's prongs and gives me the opening I need. Firing a volley of electrified punches, my fists crack rib after rib.

"AHH!" The Titan lord screams in pain.

Saturn releases one hand from the scythe, sacrificing his grapple with Neptune. With his now free hand, he swats me out of the way. I focus on summoning the winds behind me, catching myself in the air. With Saturn's attention divided, Neptune uses this opportunity to maneuver the scythe from our father's grasp.

The mighty weapon flies across the room, embedding itself into the wall. Neptune drives his trident downward and impales Saturn's forearm. At this point, Pluto makes his move. He slashes his sword, slicing a deep cut into Saturn's face. Spinning back around, Pluto flips his blade to a backhanded grip and sinks the sword into the Titan king's thigh.

"Neptune," I shout, "Douse him with water, and both of you stand back!"

Neptune summons a huge tidal wave, bigger than the mountain, and forms it into a beam directed at Saturn. The Titan, now filled with conductors and doused with water, is now ready for my attack. Neptune and Pluto, seeing my plan, step back away from Saturn. Neptune, now at a safe distance, redirects the water, forming a bubble around our father. The Titan remains still, struggling to breathe.

Calling upon the skies and nature once more, I ascend into the air. Blasting through the ceiling, the palace darkens under the storm clouds brewing. This will have to be the most powerful singular bolt of lightning I can produce. Only then can we win.

Electricity surges through my veins, pouring out of my fingertips. Lightning strikes from the clouds above. Putting all of my power into this attack, I shoot lightning from my hands. The clouds join me in my assault, merging their lightning with mine into one intense beam.

The blast connects with the bubble surrounding Saturn. Electricity pulses through the water, shocking the Titan from the outside. Simultaneously, the conductors my brothers so thoughtfully provided fry his insides. After a few seconds of this, his squirming stops.

Water splashes on the ground as Neptune releases the sphere. Saturn falls to the ground, lying limp and motionless. As the storm clouds retreat, so does the red stain. A bright blue sky and shining sun take its place.

"The war is over. You have prevailed."
Invidia appears, stepping into the destroyed room.

She motions to a nearby fireplace. Looking into the flames, the end of the battle on Olympus plays. The Olympians, my family, have defeated the Titans once more. After we lock them away in Tartarus, we can begin restoring the world.

I clap both of my brothers on the back. "We did it, my siblings. We have destroyed the wretched Titans and reclaimed our place in the cosmos."

"I guess working with you two again wasn't so bad." To my utter shock, Pluto smiles. "The reign of the Titans is officially over."

Chapter 27: World's End

After rising to the morning sun, I walk to the balcony. The view from Mount Olympus is stunning. From here, I can see not only the wartorn battlefields but the blossoming world beyond them. My tired mind starts to wander as I gaze out into the world. I begin to reminisce on the immense progress we have made since the war.

Over the last few months, the world has slowly but surely become whole again. The skies are clear, plants are blooming, and it seems even mortals have halted their assaults on each other. As far as they are concerned, this war was just a surge of natural disasters. However, for the time being, this world will know peace.

Everyone seems to have changed, and all for the better. My husband, Jupiter, has been more attentive to me. Neptune and Minerva have stopped their constant feuds. Even Pluto is in better spirits. He visits my husband and I every so often on Olympus. His relationship with Ceres has become...less hostile, though theirs is not one that can be healed overnight.

My husband and I are in preparation mode for our child. Whatever Justitia did during the final battle worked. The baby is expected to be perfectly healthy. Sometimes, when I lay awake at night, my mind wanders. I wonder what happened to the titaness of justice. Where did she end up? Elysium...or another realm entirely?

After the war, we Olympians made a pact with one another. No more petty squabbles. No more fighting over territory. From now on, we will rule in unison. We will bring prosperity and kindness to this new world.

So far, everyone has kept their word. The deities of nature work tirelessly to restore forests and other natural life around the globe. Neptune keeps his oceans calm, allowing safe passage to all voyagers and traders. Although, I can't tell if that's because of our pact or because he's busy rebuilding his palace in Atlantis.

In a surprising turn of events, Apollo gave up his duties as the sun god. He found the neutral Titan, Sol and returned the domain in full to him. Diana followed suit with Luna and her domain over the moon. If I recall correctly, they wanted to "focus their energies into their other realms." Apollo has gone on to create wondrous advancements in medicine for the mortals. Diana, on the other hand, focuses on rebuilding her followers. Unfortunately, many of them perished during the Titan assault on Olympus.

Venus and Baccus returned to their nightclub. Throughout all of this, it remained standing, with lights shining as bright as ever. It's good to keep a place where we deities can all relax and mingle woth the mortals. I've always admired their ambition, their constant nagging to get us to walk amongst mankind. It's something I plan to do more of myself after the baby.

While reminiscing on the balcony, Jupiter approaches me. "Everything alright, darling?" He puts his arms around me, lacing his fingers through mine.

"Everything is perfect, my husband." As one world ends, a new one begins. A world of love and peace. A world of rebirth and renewal. A *just* world.

INDEX

OLYMPIANS:

Jupiter/Zeus - Zeus, god of gods, is arguably the most powerful of all the Olympians. He commands the skies and, most notably, lightning.

Juno/Hera - Hera, queen of Olympus, is the goddess of marriage, childbirth, and family. Constantly scorned by her cheating husband, Zeus, Hera is also known for her revenge plots against her husband's bastard.

Neptune/Poseidon - Poseidon is one of the strongest Olympians, second only to Zeus himself. He is the god of the seas and earthquakes. He weilds a mighty trident forged by the Master Cyclopes as his main weapon.

Apollo - Apollo is the son of Zeus and Leto and twin brother to Artemis. His domain ranges through a wide assortment of realms. He is the god of medicine, archery, prophecy, and, in later years, the sun.

Diana/Artemis - Artemis, as stated above, is the twin sister of Apollo. While she also is known as an archery goddess, she too has a wide range of domains. She's the goddess of the hunt, protector of women, and the goddess of the wilderness. To mirror Apollo's sun duties, Artemis, in later years, also adopted the moon. She's usually found with her followers, a group of young nymphs, demigods, and mortals who have sworn service to the goddess. They were rarely all fighters and were even rarer to all be seen together at once.

Mars/Ares - Ares is the son of Zeus and Hera. He's the god of war, but most specifically associated with battlelust and courage.

Ceres/Demeter - Demeter is one of the original Olympian gods. She's the goddess of agriculture, bread, and grains. Although some associate her and her daughter, Persephone, with plants in general.

Proserpina/Persephone - Persephone is the daughter of Demeter and Zeus. Against her will, she was forced to marry Hades. In agreement with her mother, Demeter, she only spends 6 months of every year in the underworld with him. She, like her mother, is a plant goddess. Although Persephone is more associated with the spring.

Vesta/Hestia - Hestia is another one of the original Olympians. Although not talked about much, she is a vital member of the gods. Her domain lies with the hearth and home. She is, quite literally, the heart of Olympus.

Vulcan/Hephaestus - Hephaestus is the crippled son of Zeus and Hera. Always looked down upon by his fellow Olympians, he mainly resides in his forge, which he created inside of a volcano. He is the god of craftsmanship and forgery, building great weapons and armor for his fellow gods.

Venus/Aphrodite - Aphrodite is a bit of an odd case. Although she's always considered an Olympian, she was actually born from Uranus, a pre-mordial deity. If you were to look at the deities as generational, she would actually be a Titan. Regardless, she sits upon Olympus as the goddess of love and beauty. She was forcefully married to Hephaestus but is known for her affairs, especially with Ares.

Bacchus/Dionysus - Dionysus is the son of Zeus and Semele. He's normally seen as a drunk, being the god of wine. His domain, like many others, does not stop there. Dionysus is also the god of madness, festivity, and pleasure.

Mercury/Hermes - Hermes, son of Zeus and Maia, is the messenger of the gods. He's in charge of delivering any and all messages between the deities. On top of that, he is the god of speed, thieves, and travelers.

TITANS:

Saturn/Kronus - Kronus is the leader of the Titans and lord of time. He's the father of Zeus, Hera, Poseidon, Hades, Demeter, and Hestia. He was the one to lead the Titan revolt against his father, Uranus.

Oceanus - Oceanus is the Titan lord of the ocean. He was one of the few Titans to stay neutral during the first war against the Olympians.

Hyperion - Hyperion is the Titan lord of light. He's the father of the original sun deity Helios.

Atlas - Atlas, the lord of endurance, was kind of like the general of the Titan armies. He led the charge against the Olympians during their first war.

Justitia/Themis - Themis is the Titan deity of justice, divine law, and oracles. She was Zeus's first wife and remained on the side of the Olympians, often giving council to the king of the gods.

Invidia/Nemesis - Nemesis was the counterpart of Themis. She's the goddess of vengeance, often exacting revenge on those who committed evil.

Japetus/Iapetus - Iapetus, lord of mortality, was one of the oldest Titans. He helped Kronus and their brothers chop down their father, Uranus. He's also the father of Atlas, Prometheus, Epimetheus, and Menoitios.

Crius/Krios - Krios is the Titan lord of the stars and Constellations. He was one of the four Titan brothers who took down Uranus.

Dione/Theia - Theia is the titaness of sight and Vision. She also overlaps in the domain of light with her brother, Hyperion.

Tethys - Tethys is the titaness of fresh water. She is the wife of Oceanus.

MISC. DEITIES & CREATURES:

Pluto/Hades - Hades is the oldest son of Kronus, making him the older brother of the original Olympians. He's the ruler of the underworld of god of the dead. He's often confused as one of the Olympians but in reality, isn't one of them. He has no throne on Olympus and prefers to stay in his realm beneath the Earth.

The Fates - The Fates are three sisters that hold arguably the greatest powers in all of Greek Mythology. They weave the destiny of every deity and mortal in existence.

Empusa - Empusa are vampire-like creatures that feed on the blood and flesh of young men. They disguise themselves as beautiful women and lure the men somewhere they can devour them. Their normal form, however, consists of flaming hair and serpent-like legs.

Cyclops - A cyclops is a type of monster in Greek mythology. They are usually seen as giant, one-eyed creatures with incredible strength. Poseidon holds the most power over this breed of monster, but some are known to be excellent craftsmen and help Hephaestus at his forge.

Master Cyclopes - The Master Cyclopes are a set of specific cyclopes that helped the Olympians win the first war with the Titans. They are responsible for the creation of Zeus's master lightning bolt, Poseidon's trident, and Hades helm of darkness. Unfortunately, they were later killed in revenge by Apollo.

Satyr - Satyrs are half-goat half-human hybrids. They are creatures of nature and the wilds, often seen serving Dionysus.

Dryads - Dryads are another type of woodland creature. They are the spiritual embodiment of trees and other forest-type plants.

Letum/Thanatos - Thanatos is the closest thing Greek Mythology has to a grim reaper. While Hades is the god of the dead, Thanatos is the god of *death*. Often confused with Cupid, Thanatos has bright angelic wings and is normally depicted with either a scythe or a sword.

Manticore - A manticore is a type of hybrid monster. With the body of a lion, the tail of a scorpion, and the head of a man, the manticore is a creature to be feared far and wide.

Thank you to everyone who has purchased and read my very first novel! I hope you enjoyed this journey through the world of Gods and Titans. While I don't plan on this to start a book series, I am working on new novels, comics, and music that I believe will bring you much more enjoyment.

In the following few pages, I will give you a brief preview of my next novel ***IMMORTALITY'S CURSE: FALLEN KING***. This passage is taken from Chapter 1

Chapter 1: Dracula, The Immortal

Have you ever wished for something and had it come true? No, let me rephrase that. Have you ever gotten something you wished for but realized you didn't want it at all? If you haven't, let me tell you, it's a literal living hell.

My name is Dalv, or at least that is what I've been calling myself these days. You may know me better as Vlad. No? Then how about the infamous, immortal, all-powerful Count Dracula?! Before I became this beast, I was a human like you. Back in those days, I was dubbed "Vlad The Impaler" because I killed my Ottoman enemies by putting their worthless heads on my spears and staining the blade with the crimson-red blood that spilled from their severed heads. I would often dine in the forest of bodies created from my blood lust. When my bread was too dry, I would marinate it in their blood. A tasty treat after a long battle.

One day, on the day of my "death," my enemies finally captured me. Not something easily accomplished, might I add. They sentenced me to death by execution. Back then, that meant decapitation. Fitting, I know, being beheaded in front of the very enemies I used that same tactic on. Seconds before the blade hit my neck, I said my final curse to God. Licking the blood from the previous victim off the chopping block, I spat in the face of everything he stood for.

I believe my final act as Vlad The Impaler is what caused this curse of immortality. At first, I loved it, not being able to die and killing anyone I wished. But after centuries of seeing loved ones pass from old age, watching them shrivel away and turn to dust, I want nothing more than to go with them. I now hate my immortality. I wish it to end.

As I sit here in the darkness, recounting my past, metal chains wrap around my body, cool to the touch. My captors keep me immobile, afraid of my power. The drugs coursing through my veins, keeping me sedated and docile. The air is damp and musty.

Suddenly, the light from the hallway hits my eyes like a solar flare as my prison door is thrust open. Three men, whom I recognize all too well, enter the room. One tall and lean, blonde hair swooping over his eyes and a mischievous smile upon his pale face. Another was short, pale, and chubby with rodent-like features and greasy gray hair. He cowered behind the tall blonde. The third man was more refined. He was a middle-aged gentleman with a muscular build and short black hair. He wore a three-piece suit, implying class, but his belt and face told a different story. His face was rugged and covered with scars from previous "hunts," I'd assume, and on his belt, he carried multiple stakes, a crucifix, a revolver, and a flask of holy water.

The gentleman spoke. "So, Vla- oh, I'm sorry, you prefer Dalv now. So, Dalv, how does it feel to be captured by your enemies yet again? To be betrayed by your young apprentice?" A smirk crawled on his face.

To be continued...